Con(viction)

Con(viction)
Anthology of the Con #2

◊◊◊

edited by Erin & Colleen Garlock

Gothic City Press
Mentor on the Lake, Ohio

Compilation copyright © 2013 Gothic City Press
Introduction copyright © 2013 Gothic City Press
"Consequences" copyright © 2013 J.M. Vogel
"The Doll" copyright © 2013 Patrick Van Slyke
"Marina Waiting" copyright © 2013 Vic Warren
"Mr. Puselli's Rosebush" copyright © 2013 Jay Seate
"Origins 1995" copyright © 2013 Kathleen Molyneaux
"Pesky Psychics" copyright © 2013 Lisa Ocacio
"Preacher Con" copyright © 2013 Lyndsey Davis
"Red Cove" copyright © 2013 Michael Mohr
"Screams in the Night" copyright © 2013 J.P. Behrens
"Shelter" copyright © 2013 Leo Norman
"Skin and Bones" copyright © 2013 Kyle Yadlosky
"Whitechapel" copyright © 2013 Monica Cook

Published by
Gothic City Press
5781 Springwood Ct.
Mentor on the Lake, Ohio 44060
(440) 290-9325
www.gothiccitypress.com

First Paperback Edition
ISBN: 978-0-9852003-6-7

All rights reserved.
No part of this publication may be reproduced, stored in a retrieval system or transmitted in any form or by any means, electronic, mechanical, photocopying, recording or otherwise, without prior written permission of the publisher.

These stories are works of fiction. Names, characters, places, and incidents are either the product of the author's imagination or, if real, used fictitiously. Any resemblance to actual events, locales, or persons, living or dead, is entirely coincidental.

Coverart: "The Doll" copyright © 2013 Luke Spooner

Printed and bound in the United States of America

Contents

Introducing ... The Con _____ 10

Preacher Con _____ 13
    Lyndsey Davis

Shelter _____ 37
    Leo Norman

Whitechapel _____ 57
    Monica Cook

Skin and Bones _____ 71
    Kyle Yadlosky

Red Cove _____ 85
    Michael Mohr

Origins 1995 _____ 93
    Kathy Molyneaux

The Doll _____ 115
    Patrick Van Slyke

Marina Waiting _____ *125*
   Vic Warren

Mr. Puselli's Rosebush _____ *137*
   Jay Seate

Pesky Psychics _____ *149*
   Lisa Ocacio

Consequences _____ *163*
   J. M. Vogel

Screams in the Night _____ *185*
   J.P. Behrens

Author Bios _____ *205*

For all freaks and geeks who spend countless hours preparing for The Con, your attention to costume details, booth preparation, and everything else do not go un-noticed. We appreciate all the events, signings, games, and decorating that makes being at The Con a memorable event.

Introducing ... The Con

Welcome back to The Con. Much has happened since you were here last. The party continues back in the gaming room; three of the elves, well...attendees dressed like elves, have been negotiating with a Klingon and a Wonder Woman over how to divide their bounty from destroying the evil robot minions. The clichés continue in the vendor room with the sale of decorative swords and axes nestled in between a booth selling hand-knit monkey hats and another booth peddling fantasy-art posters from an internationally known celebrity artist sporting a neatly trimmed white beard.

We are returning to you with another batch of weird and dark tales inspired by hobbies and convention attendance. This time around, we open with an attendee and her unlikely guest, as they enjoy the treasures of San Diego Comic Con – an actual convention. We also have a second story that takes place at Origins Game Fair in Columbus, Ohio – another real life convention. Both of these stories embrace Gothic City Press' byline, "What's Your Darkness?" and lure you into the darker side of convention going, where all is not as it seems and danger masks itself as innocence.

Innocence isn't always all it's cracked up to be. In "Whitechapel" innocence hides a secret in plain sight during Victorian Era, England. On the softer side of innocence, "Shelter" explores the loss of innocence and reclaims it in Post-World War II, England. And what could be more innocent than a doll and schoolyard full of children? Don't let your guard down though, you might be surprised at how simplicity becomes complicated with the simple act of a child's kiss.

Not all ends badly for our cast of characters. Some find love in unlikely places, and not even death can break those bonds. Sometimes death makes them stronger. And therein lies the magic of the Con. For all that we endure through the normalcy of our lives, we escape into the world of The Con to make more than might otherwise be possible and to participate in the fantastic.

If you haven't attended a Con recently, grab a friend and march into the nearest Con for a weekend of fun. Be prepared to get a good dose of weird. You won't regret it.

Erin & Colleen Garlock

Preacher Con

Lyndsey Davis

Attendee: San Diego Comic Con - San Diego, California

Sally Olivia Stanton yanked on the contact points of her Deanna Troi wig, which gave her the itchies, and then, smoothed her snug maroon and black leotard. She stood in the doorway of her boutique, with cinnamon and apple aromas wafting, while she scanned her shop once more. Contrary emotions battled as she put her staff in charge of her store, a cherished entrepreneurial baby named "Remedies," so she could attend San Diego Comic Con 2013. Her display room boasted natural healing products and a host of fragrant pampering goods. The latter kept her business in the black. Sally claimed two passions: her shop and her love affair with all things Star Trek.

She waved at the preacher across the street. The mayor had introduced them at the Chamber mixer, and she'd fallen for his charm, before she learned he operated the new religious establishment. In her defense, he seemed different from every man of the cloth she'd met. Not so 'heavenly minded' and stodgy.

His church had moved to a glass enclosed storefront in the business district two weeks ago. The newsprint-covered windows displayed 'Welcome Church' in bold, crimson letters. He stopped sweeping the sidewalk in front of his church, leaned his muscular physique on the broom and returned the greeting.

"Why are you dressed like that?" Preacher Thomas Mordorne's furrowed brow didn't detract from the square jaw, high cheekbones, brown hair and an errant lock dropping over his blue eyes. His biceps bulged enough to reveal cut muscles below the sleeves of his polo shirt.

"I'm going to the San Diego Comic Con." Sally debated whether to invite him. "I'm the counselor. From Star Trek the Next Gen?"

"Like on TV or film?"

"You haven't watched Star Trek?" Sally waved bye to her staff, and strolled across to face the handsome man, not wearing a ring. "The convention is on the San Diego Magazine's Top 10 Must Do List. You should go."

"To a convention?" Tom grunted, "I wouldn't fit. My focus is on souls. Gathering souls."

"Take a day off. It'll be fun." Sally said. *He really needs to relax.*

"You may be right. Do I dress up in costume, too?" Tom winced.

"Nah. That's for Trekkies, like me."

"Trekkies?"

"Staunch fans." Sally rummaged for her keys in her oversized purse. "You don't get around much, do you?"

"Do I follow you or could we go together?" Tom's grin enchanted her.

"Please, join me." Sally grasped the remote on her key ring and called over her shoulder. "I'll wait."

Halfway across the street, Sally pressed her car-key's unlock-button and the release click sounded. She glanced around to see if he was coming.

Tom flipped the sign on the front entrance, showing "Sorry to miss you. Please come back," shut the door behind him, and jogged to catch up.

"I doubt I'll be the best for you. Though better than a substitute for your high school prom." His smile widened, white teeth contrasting with the surfer's tan.

"Don't worry. I'll guide you." Sally tossed her bulky bag into the back of her convertible, as the top slowly retracted into the trunk, and spun around. "What did you say about substitute for high school prom?"

"I would be better than someone substituting for a high school prom date." He added a wink to his grin, and she sighed a little inside.

He grabbed the handle and held her door open. She nodded her thanks and inhaled his after shave. *Wow.* Did she bat her eyes at him? She stopped a shudder and slid into the bucket seat. His athletic strut, as he skirted her car drew her attention until he sat next to her. The engine revved more than needed at the turn of the key and they drove towards the San Diego Convention Center.

"Funny you should mention. I haven't told a soul around here—my boyfriend bailed on me the night of my prom. The creep."

***

She parked in the garage, and they rode the outdoor, inclined, glass elevator up to the lobby entrance overlooking San Diego Bay. The revelry roared as soon as the automatic doors parted.

"How huge." Tom hesitated. "Although, I'm used to crowds."

Sally tugged his arm and dragged him through registration and soon they were strolling the booths, past Darth Vaders and Wonder Women, Ironmen and Hellboys.

"The guy in red."

"He's dressed as Hellboy." Sally shrugged. "He's a demon turned good. Grinds down his horns."

"A demon turned good? Impossible." Tom shook his

head. "Such false teaching."

"It's a story. A comic book. Not real." Sally chuckled and air quoted around 'story' and 'not real.'

"But what people read leaves a mark on their soul. I look for souls, and I recognize, when they are…needy."

"You're off the clock, Preacher man."

"I'm never off the clock."

"Relax. Have some fun."

"I think what I do is fun."

"Just an expression. Not a judgment." Sally pulled him aside to examine the convention program. "Yay! A chance to meet Marina Sirtis at the Light Speed booth #3745. They're signing! OMG! Jonathan Frakes, Brent Spiner and Michael Dorn, too. We gotta go now."

"Uh who?"

"No matter. Just follow." She kicked her speed walking into high gear, reaching behind her for his hand. They maneuvered around crowds to the booth. They were late. The signing would start at ten o'clock. Her heart dropped when she assessed the number of Trekkies that had gathered. They slipped in behind Worf and Lt Uhura lookalikes. An overly tall Mr. Data and a plump Captain Janeway boxed them from behind.

"Now what?" Tom's eyes flickered around the arena and returned to meet hers.

"We wait."

"How long?"

"A couple of hours."

"Two hours? Won't you miss the rest of the convention?" Tom cocked his head. "Why pay so much to stand in line?"

"It'll be three and a half before we get to the front for signatures." Sally pulled a collapsible stool out of her oversized bag. "I didn't have two, but we can take turns."

"I don't mind staying. You go and check things out. Besides, there are souls right here."

"Comic Con is not a place to proselytize. You can't do stuff here without a license and a booth."

"I'll be subtle. I always am." Tom grinned. "Go on. Have 'fun'."

"I can't. It's against the rules. No saving spots, except for bathroom breaks."

"I'll take care of it. No one'll even be aware."

"Are you sure? I don't need the place-saver-police arresting me."

"Absolutely. It won't be like a college prankster getting caught by the dean." Tom wiggled his eyebrows. "This is an opportunity for me."

"How villainous of you." Sally handed him the canvas stool, turned to walk away, but stopped and spun around. "What did you say about getting caught by the dean?...How did you hear...?"

Tom had already begun talking to Worf and Uhura and didn't respond. With a frown, she headed to the conference room, where the latest Star Trek movie actors shared a stage panel and answered questions.

Two hours later, she returned with sodas, chips and gyros. "Are you hungry?"

"I could eat." Tom accepted the food and offered her the seat.

She dropped her bag and settled on the canvas stool. "Thanks. The line has moved about halfway. You're right, no one seems to mind you saved a spot for me."

"No, I've been having quite a time getting to know people."

Sally checked the faces surrounding them and their

energetic chatting suggested that Tom hadn't spoiled the day. At least they weren't glaring at her for him saving her a place. Tom's charisma at work. *All that gorgeousness wasted in a church.* When they finished eating, they scooted forward with the crowd.

"Is this your friend?" a southern twang behind them interjected.

"Yes, Mary Lou, meet Sally. She sells soaps and herbs across the street from my Welcome Church."

"You must be lucky with someone like Preacher, here." Mary Lou, as Captain Janeway, tugged on a tall Mr. Data behind her. "Jeremy and I are so excited to meet him. We're gonna visit his services, before we head back to Texas."

Sally arched her eyebrow at Tom and mouthed: *Take the day off.*

"Talking. Just talking. Wouldn't you know they are interested in what I offer?"

"What did you offer them?" Sally moved, when the line inched forward.

"Everything." He winked like they shared in a conspiracy.

"I just love your Counselor Troi outfit." Mary Lou nodded her head, as if her statement needed confirming.

"I have a Captain Janeway uniform, too. Isn't it fun?" *I can't possibly say I love hers. She looks like the Pillsbury doughboy was stuffed into Janeway's tunic and stretch pants. Focus on the eyes and don't laugh.*

"We had trouble finding Mr. Data clothes in a size as tall as Jeremy." Mary Lou prattled on.

Sally admired the thoroughness of the consistent color on his hands, face and neck. "Does greasepaint take long to put on? You did a fantastic job."

"Mary Lou applies the make-up for me." Jeremy-Mr. Data replied. "Her forte, not mine."

Sally smiled at Mary Lou's 1970s coif and blue eye shadow, and could only nod like a bobble head doll. Her mind blanked on anything more to add and so she pivoted to face forward, stepping on the heel of the person in front.

"Oh, excuse me. I didn't mean to..." Sally lurched to the side and the couple turned.

"No matter, dearie. Hi Tom. This your friend?" Worf and Uhura grinned.

"Sally. Sally O. Stanton" she offered her hand and gripped theirs in a firm shake.

"We recognize you, Counselor Troi. Tom told us all about you and your healing boutique." Mable's voice sounded more Data-like and mechanical. "We want to experience his church, before we go back to Minnesota, and we'll visit your store, too. I love those good smelling soaps. We told him we'd help him get connected to our list of Star Trek followers. Such an amazing vision for his church."

"How..." Sally searched for the correct words, but settled on, "...delightful."

The couple turned to each with googly eyes.

Sally leaned back, bumping Tom's solid chest, and dropped her voice. "Do they seem...odd?"

"No. Quite typical." Tom dismissed her concerns.

"Why do I get the Stepford wife image when I talk with them?"

"Stepford?"

"Don't you watch any TV? Stepford Wives—a movie where mind controlled spouses serve their husbands like automatons."

"Never had TV."

The line lessened until Sally failed at not gushing in front of Marina Sirtis, who complimented her costume and hair. She pointed to the stall selling the new Build-a-Bridge bobble head dolls.

With photos signed, the two neighbors moved around the arena, filling Sally's bag with freebies. Tom relented and bought a messenger tote that displayed the Comic Con 2013 logo. She stowed her secret treasures, silly additions to her collection of Star Trek memorabilia. Everywhere they lingered, Tom worked his magnetism and they ended up with more than average bounty.

Exhaustion set in, and they called it quits for the day. The drive home was quiet and they returned to their shops very late.

"Thanks for inviting me. Such a profitable day." Tom saluted with his middle index finger. Sally covered her recoil, as best as possible.

Get out much? "You're welcome. Um, I don't know how to say this, but you don't use the third finger to say hi and goodbye. It's not ..." Sally faltered, hunting for words.

"Oh. Where I'm from..." Tom's winsome smile relaxed her.

"I'm going back tomorrow, if you want a ride."

"On Sunday? My big day? No. Thanks, though." Tom's allure never failed to please.

The next morning, dressed in her Captain Janeway outfit, Sally saw a line of congregants had formed across the street at Welcome Church. Many resembled the attendees at the booths from yesterday.

He sold them well if they are giving up the last day of Comic Con to attend church. A packed house—quite the following for a startup. Odd.

Sally spent the day jostling her way to favorite events and booths. She filled her bag with goodies and a complete set of original Star Trek-The Next Generation Build-a-Bridge bobble heads. Weary upon arriving at home, she parked and unpacked her car, making several trips upstairs to her apartment over the shop.

The Welcome Church's lights illuminated the boulevard. The congregation's voices, in rap and song, spilled through the cracks. She crept across the street to peek through the slivers of light among the paper-covered windows. The room throbbed with gyrating bodies, raising their hands and swaying to the beat.

Not like any church I ever went to.

"You can come inside."

Sally lurched backwards, nearly falling. "You scared me. Why aren't you in with your followers?"

"Your shadow drew my attention and I came to invite you."

"Has the crowd been here all day?"

"Time flies...."

"All day? What are you feeding them? Drugs?"

"Better than that. I give them what they want." Tom grinned. "Come on in, but I warn you, your life will change."

"Uh..eerm...I kinda had a bad experience with a church judging me for selling stuff that they thought was New Age and had to do with witches." Sally backed away. "I think not."

The plump Mary Lou stepped through the door, "Tom? You're needed."

"Mary Lou? Remember me? Comic Con 2013? Yesterday? In line?" Sally moved toward the woman.

"Are you okay?... Just a no make-up day?"

"Oh yes, how are you Sally?" Mary Lou's bright eyes of yesterday now appeared glazed as if she suffered from cataracts.

Yowza! Without makeup you take on a ghostly tinge—dark shadows circle your eyes, like wearing two chocolate donut monocles.

Mary Lou's neck twisted oddly, as she turned to Tom, and with a sing song voice said, "We're wait-ing."

"Mary Lou? Are you okay? You don't look…uh…" *There was no way to say it delicately. Her appearance was downright spooky.*

"Fine dearie." Mary Lou answered, without turning toward Sally.

"Fine? Dearie? What happened to your Texas accent?" A chill ran up Sally's spine and a shiver radiated down her arms and legs. "What's going on? …Tom?"

"Everything is fine, Sally. Come on in and join us. We offer unmatched experiences."

The sound of laughter swelled and poured into the street, when Mary Lou's lanky husband opened the door and poised under the jambs. "You're missing the fun."

"Fun? Church?" Sally scoffed. "Not a believer. But this, I gotta see."

Mary Lou grabbed one arm and Tom, the other, propelled her forward. Their fingers would leave marks where they touched Sally's tender skin.

"You won't ever want to depart." Mary Lou dug deeper into Sally's upper arm.

"Ouch. You're hurting me. Can you lighten up?" She was close enough to Mary Lou's husband to recognize his eyes shared the same sunken countenance of his wife's. "I changed my mind. Maybe later. I...I...I just remembered my mom is expecting me to call her tonight and tell her about Comic Con 2013."

Tom nodded to Mary Lou and they both released Sally. She retreated back to her car, locked it and stumbled up to her apartment.

"What just happened?" She spoke to the empty room. The creepies climbed up and down her spine for the next hour and she poured herself a glass of red wine. The swirling of the Merlot on her tongue and its trickle down her throat allowed her to savor the full taste and warmth. After half a bottle, she stumbled to bed and drifted into sleep.

The alarm woke her and she wiped the drool off her mouth and cheek. Her morning Yoga routine required twice as long to unkink her body. The brutality of two days of walking, drinking too much, and sleeping in an awkward position had taken a toll.

She showered, but the warmth failed to calm her. Shivers continued to remind her that her Spidey sense screamed "Wrong."

"Tom is such a nice guy." *That's what all the neighbors say about serial killers. And those people couldn't have been sweeter at the convention. Why do they all have sunken eyes now? Why give up a day at Comic Con? And who would find spending all that time at church...'fun?' Call Mom.*

She grabbed her cell and punched the number one on speed-dial and slumped to her sofa, her knees bouncing up and down with rapid nervous energy.

"Mom?" Sally gulped. "I'm fine. No. Really. Can't a girl call her mother?...not on a Monday without alarming you?" She breathed deeply and rattled off the events of

Comic Con, neglecting to mention her neighbor or the weird evening.

"So. Darling. What are you not telling me?"

Her mom grew up on the streets of Brooklyn. That savvy street smarts never left Maria, no matter how long she'd lived in San Francisco.

"Nothing."

"Yeah. A lotta nothing adds up. So. Wh-at?" Her New York twang soothed Sally's fears. She trusted her mother, the cynic, to raise excellent questions.

"My neighbor, the preacher. Thomas Mordorne, and his followers. Or converts." Sally shared the events of Comic Con and the weird vibes she received from Mary Lou and her husband, adding the church service went all day, until their eyes became hollow.

"You get what you pay for." The sound of chomping gum between words took Sally back to her mom's kitchen, where long chats and confidences were exchanged. She could almost smell the snicker doodles, bought from an upscale bakery and the potpourri of cinnamon and cloves.

"I didn't pay for anything."

"Just saying. He's a weird one. Not buying the spiel." Maria added, "Check the back door, the garbage, and who leaves. Garbage speaks the real truth. Better than a pulpit."

"It's probably nothing, but the hair on my neck is prickling."

"Trust yourself. I taught you well. Just because you don't do church now—those prejudicial idiots—doesn't mean you didn't learn right and wrong as a child." Maria paused. "You need I should come down?"

"No. Not necessary. I can fight my own battles."

"Of course. I gave you the best education, not that I'm a Jesus freak or anything."

"Thanks, Mom. Gotta go. Love ya." Sally hung up.

She appreciated her mom's simple approach. Her knees stopped bouncing, and Sally took a deep breath and sighed. She resumed getting organized and hurried to open the store.

Instead of puttering in the office, Sally roamed the sales floor. Throughout the day, her eyes strayed to the building across the street, as she feigned working.

No one went in or out. The lack of activity contrasted with the liveliness of the day before.

Dusk shifted to night and Sally changed to jeans and a hoody. Armed with a flashlight and her cellphone, she snuck out to the alley and jogged around two blocks, to be certain the driveway was empty around the church dumpster. She lifted the plastic hood and shined the light on several neatly tied bags. As the stench of rotting food hit her, dinner leapt from her stomach and burned the back of her throat.

A sound at the rear entrance alerted her and she ducked behind the big metal bin. Shoes crunched on gravel. No peeking now. In fact, her heart pounded so loud she feared the unknown person might hear. Her concentration to slow her respiration required effort. She inhaled and held her breath, while the steps halted in front of the dumpster. The cover squeaked when the visitor opened it and deposited a bag. The lid thumped down and the individual retreated. Diminishing sounds gave her courage enough to lean around the corner. She caught a glimpse of a figure wearing a long cape and a hood entering the back door.

Someone actually wore a hooded cape to empty the

garbage? Crazy. Sally crawled from her hiding spot and lifted the lid, removing the last deposit of trash. The tie was loosely twisted, leaving the contents exposed. Comic Con goodies. *Oh my god! These are new. Unopened. Memorabilia. Hundreds, maybe, thousands of dollars' worth.*

Another bag revealed similar treasures. More Comic Con collectables. She tucked the bags back and raced around the block to her car. Driving as close as she could, but still keeping her car hidden from the church door, she opened the lid and grabbed the treasures. Her car bulged with stowed bags.

She drove to her alley and transferred the bounty via the back entrance to her apartment. Two trips produced over a dozen bags. The remaining dumpster debris consisted of the usual scraps of paper, pizza boxes, soda cans—they obviously didn't recycle or care about the earth—and a bag of shredded material. Like ripped up clothes? Why would a church have ripped up clothes? She'd examine that later.

Her apartment overflowed with the smell of garbage smeared on the outside of bags, despite the protected mint quality souvenirs inside. She stacked the still-in-the-box unopened toys on one table, which overflowed to the floor. The broken, but repairable, souvenirs filled one corner of the table. Stuff like it sold on eBay all the time. She collected the broken-and-unusable memorabilia in the used bags. She emptied the last bag of strips of material piled up on her dining table.

What a find! She boogied in the small square of open floor, and froze with her arms in a victory pose. A niggling voice at the back of her head asked, "Why would the church throw out all that good merchandise?"

The phone rang.

"Hello."

"Hi Sally. Tom, here. How are you?"

Oh my god. Did he see me? "Hi Tom. What can I do for you? It's late."

"Yes. I wondered if you found it." Tom's easy voice lured her.

"Found what?"

"What you were looking for."

"What are you talking about?" Sally's heart beat louder. Could he hear it over the phone?

"You can't lie to me." Tom's voice deepened and dropped to a whisper.

"Lie? About what?" Sally laughed, but it sounded like a guilty giggle.

"I saw you. Behind the dumpster."

"What? What are you talking about?"

"The toys. The memorabilia. They're evil."

"Tom, you're mistaken..." Sally sat up at the 'evil' word and chuckled. "I don't believe in evil."

"Sally," Tom's timbre resonated through the phone and Sally shivered.

"Wha-at?" Irritation rising, she was about to read him the riot act. How dare he use that parental disciplinary voice with her?

"You're curious. You checked the dumpster and took bags in your car. You're sorting them now."

"How... What... Are you spying on me?" Sally's tone rose in volume as Tom's decreased.

"I know you, Sally. I know your likes and dislikes. I'm here for you. Come on over to the door and I'll let you in. Let's talk."

"I'm not coming over at this hour. It's late. I have to

open the shop early." Sally's voice reached the shrill level.

"I put the mementos in the bags and left them there for you. I expected you to be curious."

"How do you know that?" She might have squeaked on the last word.

"I am privy to your life, Sally. I'm across the street. I have eyes."

"I gotta go. Good. Bye. Tom." *I have eyes on you, too, Buster. Does bravado ever work?* She hung up and clasped her hands together to stop the shaking. The shivers had moved in. What had she gotten herself into?

The half bottle of merlot called to her and she poured a glass and changed for bed. While she sipped, a late night show entertained her with celebrity ghost experiences. The host spoke of goose bumps on his arms.

"You got nothing on me." She yelled at the TV. The hairs on her arms and neck stood high, in agreement. Despite her edginess, she dropped off to sleep.

Her dreams played out scenes starring bobble headed actors. Wobbling heads waddled in their Star Trek uniforms. Sally's bobble head face wore her Counselor Troi uniform, and when she encountered the Marina Sirtis bobbing doll, they argued.

"How dare you presume to be me? You're not me." Sirtis's bouncing head shrieked at Sally's.

"It's fun. It's just for fun. Overly possessive, much?"

"Not fun when people use me for evil." Counselor Troi doll lisped.

"What's with the 'evil' today?" Sally's exasperation mounted.

"Check them. Filled with…Ev-il."

"Now you're sounding like the church lady. Stop it."

"Check them."

"How am I supposed to check them?"

The alarm rang and Sally lifted weary lids. Her body ached like she hadn't slept in a week. Had she slept? Getting ready for work dragged on her energy and she fixed a double espresso, and added cold water so she could chug it. She rubbed her shoulders and her chest over the heart, where she felt a tightening.

What's wrong with you? Sally stretched and held her yoga stances. The relentless pressure on her chest worried her.

She stumbled to the bathroom, her eyes barely focused, and downed a couple of pain killers, when the doorbell interrupted.

Preacher Tom. Handsome. Rested. Smiling. *How does he manage to look like he's off to a modeling gig at zero dark thirty in the morning?*

"What's with the early rise bell?" Sally didn't invite him in, not with the increasing vibe that said stay away. Hadn't her mom remind her to pay attention to her gut?

"Come with me, Sally."

"I'm not coming with you."

"I have something you'll want to see. I made it for you."

Sally wasn't about to go, but the tightening increased in her chest. Though part of her said "NO!" she found herself relenting. She couldn't explain why. A pressure to go overwhelmed her. *Where did that come from?*

The tightening increased and her reluctance dissipated. "Okay, but I gotta come back and open up soon."

"You'll like it." Tom assured. "You should wear your Commander Troi costume."

Sally whipped her head around, "How did you know she was a commander? I thought you said you didn't know Star Trek."

"I'll wait."

"Wait for what?"

"For you to change into your costume."

"I'm not putting it on." That pressure again on her throat and heart, insisting she wear the uniform. Sally shook her head, but discovered she was unable to resist. "Okay. Wait a minute."

She returned, wearing the Star Trek two-piece Commander Troi plunging neckline tunic with pants. Although discomfort filled her, she replicated the Stepford wives' manners. A panic that she'd lost control suffused her. "Let's get this over."

He opened the door of the church, and she entered first, but when the lights flipped on, she froze. Stunned.

"Looks good, doesn't it?" Tom asked.

The room. The Bridge. Like a Star Trek the Next Generation stage. Costumed Trekkies populated the set, their heads bobbing like their bobble head counterparts.

"What is this?" Sally shut her mouth, but the lower jaw kept dropping.

"I built this for you." Tom said.

"I don't get why." Sally strolled among the people with bobbing heads, recognizing the Trekkies she met at Comic Con. Bodies stiff, their heads moved, but their eyes remained vacant.

"I told you. The bobble heads were evil. They hold the spirits of these people. They sold them to me."

"What the...? Who the hell are you?"

"That's fairly accurate. Unlike that imposter, Hellboy, I am a true demon. I give people what they want and they follow me. Now, this is where you pay."

"Me? Pay? What are you talking about?"

"You stole the bobble heads with the spirits in them. They have infected you. That's why you feel pressure to do what they suggest."

"You're crazy. You can't be a demon."

"Some might feel that way, but in fact, demons aren't ugly and unsightly. We're rather dashing and we lure people by our charisma."

"I haven't sold anything to you."

"You let me in."

"I never let you in. I don't believe in you."

"I recognized that about you. Your mom. Savvy woman. She taught you to be suspicious. I used that. Lured you to my dumpster, where I loaded the very thing you could not resist. The memorabilia of Comic Con. The bobble heads filled with the spirits controlled by evil. I told you the truth. Truth can be used by demons. We don't need to lie. I just misdirected you."

"But I haven't sold myself to you."

"No. But you allowed me to fill your life with my spirits."

"I'm just as free as I was before."

"No you aren't. You can't leave here."

"Of course, I can." The tightening in her throat and chest paralyzed Sally for a moment, before she could inhale.

"Trouble breathing?"

"Only a little pressure. No doubt, I'm ripe for a heart attack." *Don't be flippant. He's crazy. You have no idea what he might do.*

"Those are the spirits at work. You invited them into your home. I control them. They influence, to the point of controlling you. If you try to leave, they can strangle you."

"I don't believe you." But the pressure grew tighter. "All right. What do you want?"

"You must sign your soul over to me. I gather souls. I told you."

"How do I do that?"

"You sign here." Tom laid a parchment down on Spock's console, where a glass inkwell with a red liquid and quill rested. He pointed to post-it tags for her signature and initials. "You'll need to initial your S.O.S."

"I don't sign anything until I have read it all, and had my lawyer review it, too." Sally snapped back.

"There is no negotiating."

"Negotiation is my business. You think I have the best prices because suppliers give it away?" Sally stood. "I'm going back to my house and I want to call my lawyer. Then I will come back. I promise."

"You think I'm stupid?"

"No. But you want a binding deal."

"I've bound you already."

"Nope. You haven't or you would not be asking me to sign."

"Okay. I'll let you go for a few hours. Open your store and call your lawyer."

Sally strode over to her building and up the stairs to her apartment. She picked up the phone and dialed her attorney. While she listened to the ring, she reached for a bobble head and shattered it on the hard wood. A wisp rose.

The counsel's answering service kicked in and she left a message. She slammed another head on the floor.

She punched #1 on her speed dial and smashed two

more bobble heads. With each crash, a faint mist hovered and dissipated. Her mother failed to answer.

The tension constricting her chest loosened with each memento she decimated, until none remained to throw. Sweeping up the bits into bags, ceramic shards filled her trash. Then she vacuumed the remaining dust and emptied it into her dumpster.

"Can you tighten my throat and heart?" Sally spat her words towards the window overlooking the church.

No response. She punched the incoming call list on her phone and scrolled to Tom's number. He answered before it rang once.

"Still feeling the power?" She used her commanding, snarky voice.

"Just because you smashed them all, doesn't mean I don't have power over you."

"There's no tightening of my throat now.

"I can tighten your throat."

"So what? I can bind your power."

"I'm not weak. I'm a lot stronger than you."

"Yeah. You're probably stronger than me. But the irony is that I learned an important lesson from you."

"What's that?"

"You kept saying there is evil. I didn't believe you. Now, I've seen the lure of evil first hand. You manipulated me. You snagged the souls in the bobble heads. You convinced me. Evil exists. I never believed my mom, or my catechism classes, because I didn't believe there was evil."

"So what. Big deal. Evil exists. You could have seen it all around you but you didn't." Tom chuckled. "You were begging for me to control your life."

"On the contrary, you taught me evil does exist.

Therefore, so must the opposite. What I learned about choosing between serving God or the devil must be true. Therefore, I believe Jesus was right. I confess Jesus as Lord. I ask forgiveness. And, Tom? In the name of Jesus. With the power of Jesus, I bind your spirit."

The line went dead.

Shelter

Leo Norman

Attendee: Dimension Jump - London, England

We moved into the house on Asphodel Drive at the end of the spring. A friendly, detached bungalow on a good street, outside the rush of inner-city living; we couldn't have been happier. A prefab, the estate agent told us, trying not to catch my eye. Factory-built to house the post-war homeless. He needn't have worried. This kind of detail piqued my interest. I did my research; found the whole street had been reduced to a crater during the blitz. Asphodel Drive had been erected to paper over the cracks early in 1946. But the past, like the lingering stench of burning cities, refused to be forgotten.

Half drowning in heavy April rain, I lifted the last box from the boot of the car and made a dash for the front door. The single storey building squatted in the mud of its neglected front garden. Painted bright pink, in line with the other brightly coloured houses of the street, the gloss was beginning to peel from the precast concrete panels.

"It's a Unity," the estate agent had revealed. "Precast concrete over metal joists."

Mary liked the name Unity. Said it made her feel like we were part of something. Not so isolated as in the city.

"It's always the same," agreed the agent. "The more people, the less they want to know."

With a little pressure from my shoulder the front door popped open, and I staggered inside. I dumped the box onto the pile and entered the Kitchen where Mary sipped her tea.

"What do you think?" I asked.

She smiled; an expression she had rarely exhibited over the last year. "It's perfect."

I made an exaggerated show of looking around. "Even though the paint is peeling, the plaster's crumbling and the carpets are rotten?"

"Because of that."

I smiled. She was right. This was what we needed. A fresh start. A project. We needed to build a home, and this place felt right.

"Can you imagine how the first family must have felt?" She asked. "Their house destroyed by bombs and then this just pops up from the ashes."

"Like a phoenix."

"Yes. Like a phoenix, James! That's perfect. A phoenix for a fresh start. "

We stood in silence. Mary sipping her tea, smiling—the old wall clock ticking out time. I wondered if it was original.

"We'll call it Phoenix House!" Mary suddenly blurted.

I nodded. Phoenix House. Life after death.

***

We lived out of boxes while men came to look at the house and patch her up. Each would tut and shake their heads as if we had been mad to buy the place, but the work went well; crumbling plaster was replaced, faded exterior paint updated, a leaky roof mended. Meanwhile, Mary worked like a woman possessed; painted interior walls, ripped up carpets, applied bleach to everything.

"Don't you want a break?" I asked, looking up from my coffee. She'd had me ripping up skirting boards and replacing them with pre-cut sheets from the local timber yard. Joints aching but job done, I settled down in my old armchair and thought about reading the paper.

"No, that's okay," Armed with burnt orange paint, Mary carefully touched up the edges of a "feature wall" in the dining room. I couldn't help feeling that all walls were features, but kept my views to myself. "Why don't you start on the garden?"

I looked at the paper, then out the window. More drizzle.

"Sounds great."

***

Buttoning my coat, I stepped out into the drizzle. Out-of-control hedges flanked a garden dominated by weeds and nettles. A tree, old but not old enough to have seen the war, occupied the centre of the garden. It was bare. Leafless. I wondered whether it was dead.

The back end of the garden was the worst of all. Thick bramble grew over rubble. A mass of thorns. I looked at my hands. I would need gloves for this one. And something sharp.

Back inside, Mary was still painting. I hadn't seen her like this since... well, it had been a long time. She bent, picked up the pot of paint and dipped her small edging brush into it. She looked as if she were about to paint a masterpiece. No. She was a masterpiece; red hair draping in ringlets across her shoulders, slender but not frail figure, delicate fingers with nails just beginning to grow back. The lines of care under her eyes disappeared in an absent smile.

I smiled, turned and rummaged through a nearby box. Before long I had my old gardening gloves and my weapon of choice: gardening shears. It took me two days to clear the garden. I chopped and I hewed and I dug. My hands blistered. My muscles burned. At night I flexed my new found biceps and Mary laughed before beckoning me into bed.

On the third evening, we stood in the garden with a million stars over us and watched the small bonfire burn. Mary toasted our hard work, overflowing my glass with champagne. It was a clear night and, even with my woolly hat pulled down low, an icy wind bit at the exposed flesh of my cheeks.

I looked around the garden, admired the totality of my shrubbery extermination. Nothing living survived. We stood on sheets of MDF and crushed packing boxes we'd laid over the frozen ground. Soon our toes were numb. Leaving Mary daydreaming by the fire, I soon found myself tugging at the debris I'd unearthed under the brambles. The rubble danced in the orange light of the fire, casting long shadows against the high rear wall.

I picked up a small piece of rubble and held it to the light. An old chunk of brick, mortar still clinging to it. Not interesting in itself. Except these houses were all built of concrete panels.

"Stop obsessing about those rocks, James," whispered Mary, wrapping an arm around my waist. "This is it. The first stage is over. We've made this house a home."

I felt the heft of the brick in my hand, then lobbed it into the fire. Tonight was for celebration. Tomorrow, I would investigate the debris.

***

It wasn't until midday that I managed to get out to the garden.

When the sun burst, unwelcome, into our bedroom

that morning, I peered, bleary eyed, at the alarm clock. 05.52. Yet somehow we slept in, pillows pulled firmly over our heads, backs turned to the window. Then, breakfast in bed. Coffee, crumpets smothered in butter, and two aspirins each. We watched the dross of daytime television, the set perched on one of the last packing boxes.

"It feels strange to feel so content," said Mary.

I nodded, but couldn't let go of the garden and the mystery I felt could be buried there.

Soon Mary was up and looking for the curtain rail, and I was pulling on my boots, my winter jacket, hat and gloves.

"Have fun, dear," called Mary as I shut the door.

I began by piling up all the smaller, loose pieces in my wheelbarrow and transporting them to the skip out the front of the house. The heap grew smaller and I moved onto bigger pieces. I could move only one or two at a time without the wheel sinking into the mud.

"Getting anywhere?" Mary called from the doorway.

I looked up at her mischievous smile and grunted. I was tired and my back ached, but I couldn't give up. Not now.

The sun started dropping in the sky before I came to the last, huge piece of rubble. It was part of a wall and must have been four foot square. I found an edge and heaved. The veins in my neck bulged but the chunk of wall didn't budge. I tried levering it up with my spade. It bent at the handle.

I glared at it, panting, and sat down on the wheelbarrow. To get so close and fail... Angry, I threw the ruined spade into the gloom of the garden. There had to be a way.

Mary would have told me to wait until tomorrow. Get some help. We have forever to move it. Well, this time Mary would have been wrong. I had to move it. Now.

I went back into the house and grabbed my largest hammer. It wasn't perfect, but it was heavy enough. It would do. Back outside, I swished it back and forth, rehearsing my stroke.

"You should probably protect your eyes if you really want to do that." Mary appeared out of the semidarkness, handing me the plastic goggles from my toolbox. She gave me a knowing look and retreated to the back door but didn't go in.

"Are you really going to watch this?"

"I want to see my big cave man smash up some rocks!"

I grinned. "Cave man smash! Ugg! Ugg!"

I lifted the hammer and brought it down in a wide arc. A huge, angry recoil travelled up my arm. My teeth chattered and my eyeballs shook. A few tiny chips of brick flew. I felt a dash of disappointment but the brick *had* cracked. I set about it, blow after blow. Each long, angry swipe brought a shower of sparks and brick shards, some of which pinged off my goggles. Chunks of the wall crumbled and soon I was able to pick up the last large segment and waddle, bent kneed, to the wheelbarrow.

"What's that?" Mary shone her torch past me, back at the space I'd just left. I carefully dumped the wall segment into the wheelbarrow and turned.

There was a round hatch in the ground.

"Sewage outlet?" I pondered.

"I don't think so. I don't think anybody has seen that hatch in over sixty years. The Water Board must have looked at our pipes during that time."

I stood, staring at it. A blacker circle in the black night.

"Perhaps it's an air raid shelter," I said, eyes still locked onto the hatch. My heart pounded.

Mary punched me playfully on the shoulder. "Well, look at you. You got your mystery!" She smiled. "Now, if you don't mind, I'm going to make dinner. It's late."

My eyes never left the black void. I could feel it drawing me in. I needed to know what was down there. I needed to get inside.

"I might just prise this open first," I murmured.

Mary was already gone. Her silhouette pottered about in the kitchen.

Down on my knees, I ran my hands over the metal plate. At some point, I had slipped off my gloves. The hatch was rough with rust. How did it open? There was no handle. I laid my hands on it, pushed. Nothing. Ran my palms, open-handed across it in one direction, then another. Tiny splinters of rusted iron pierced my skin. It didn't matter. All that mattered was getting this thing open. Down there was the past, a bubble in time. I banged my fist on the hatch in frustration. How was it supposed to open?

It was really dark now. Mary had left the torch sitting by the wheelbarrow. Bending to pick it up, I remembered the broken spade. I placed the blade into the crack around the hatch and pushed hard with my foot. It went in with surprising ease. I took the bent handle in my hands and heaved it backwards, attempting to lever the hatch away from the surface. It moved. A sigh of long dead air escaped the black mouth of a long forgotten entrance. A smell like rotten vegetables and garlic filled my nostrils.

I gave one last jerk and the hatch flipped back, clattering onto the wooden board behind. I was in.

***

I awoke, shivering, and reached for the duvet. It wasn't there. Disorientated, my gritty eyes blinked open to reveal I had fallen asleep on the sofa. The previous night slowly came back to me. My battle to open the grate. What followed.

I put one chapped, dirty palm to my forehead and brushed a strand of spider's web from my eyes. More of the previous night returned to me and I shuddered. Thank God I got there first.

I crept into the bathroom, filled the sink with warm water. Peering into the darkness of the mirror, I expected a face to loom behind me. But there was nothing. Just my own tired face and the early morning gloom.

I worked up a soapy lather, splashed water in my face and went back to bed.

The half-sleep I fell into was filled with dreams but when I woke again, Mary having jerked open her newly erected curtains. All I could remember was fear and the horrible sense of recognition.

"Good morning, Indie."

"Huh?"

"My own adventurer cum archaeologist. My hero!" She swooned onto the bed in mock appreciation, then wrapped an arm around my neck and kissed me. "Find anything exciting?"

"It's all pretty interesting. I don't think anyone has been down there since the war." This wasn't true. I knew someone had. "Lots of old 1940s bits and bobs down there. You'd like it."

We both lay there, staring at the ceiling. "I'll have to

Shelter

pop down after breakfast and have a look. Sounds fun!"

My heartbeat lost its rhythm for a moment and I took a deep breath. *Calm, James. Calm.* I let the breath out slowly and quietly before speaking. "Make it after lunch. It's filthy and could be quite dangerous. Let me clear it up a bit first."

Mary turned her head so that we were both looking directly into each other's eyes.

"My knight in shining armour. They said chivalry was dead." She smiled. It seemed to be coming so naturally to her now. Why couldn't I smile back? "Next thing I know, you'll be holding the car door open for me."

"Don't push it," I said, pulling the duvet over my head.

After a hastily consumed breakfast, I returned to the air-raid shelter. It was closed. I couldn't remember closing the hatch, but my whole exit was a blur. Trusty spade in hand, I reopened it and peered inside.

Last night, it had felt like the darkness of the hole was solid; that I could have reached out and touched it or even stepped on it and not fallen. Now the dark gave way to the light, revealing rough, earthy sides and an ancient wooden ladder. Last night I had clambered down eagerly, foolishly, but now I kicked at the top rung, then knelt and shook it violently. The ladder was cold and dry. I could see the tiny holes that signalled woodworm, but it felt firm enough.

I placed one foot on a rung, then the other. I leant on the mouth with my arms, gripping the soil with one hand and my torch with the other. From ground level, the house looked bigger. More imposing. *It's just shadows and the past.*

I began my descent. The temperature dropped and the pungent, garlicky stench grew. The walls narrowed, closer and closer. My heart raced faster with each darkening step. *Just shadows.* I had to force each foot down. One step. Another. Then a sharp crack. A rung sagged in the middle and buckled under my foot.

I clung to the ladder, panting, eyes clamped shut.

Nothing else happened. I took another downward step, realised I had reached the bottom and let go of the ladder. The broken rung was fifteen centimetres off the ground.

"Just shadows and the past." The words echoed around the long-abandoned room and came back sounding hollow.

I lifted the torch. The space was no bigger than the box room in the bungalow. The earth of the walls and the ceiling were held in place by large wooden beams. The ground had once been carpeted but all that was left were a few rags over the musty earth.

The harsh beam of light illuminated an old wooden table bearing a dusty plate with something congealed on it. Wax. As if a candle had been allowed to burn away to nothing. Sweeping the light across the room, I picked out more archaeological treasures: some tin cans (Hereford Corn Beef, Squadron Leader Tobacco); dusty glass bottles; an empty lantern; a couple of dusty, rotten books. All the time, I avoided the corner. No need to go there. Yet.

The room had been dark for a long, long time. Nooks and crannies reluctantly gave way to the light. The darkness, returning after the torch passed, was darker and more sinister than before. As I sucked at the unwholesome, putrid air, I felt I was standing in a tiny cell; an oubliette.

The torch alighted on something I hadn't noticed the night before. A scraggly, brown heap. A mess of fur.. I stooped and picked it up. Turning it over, two dead, glassy eyes stared at me. It was wearing the remnants of a tiny red jacket.

A teddy bear. I clutched it tight, a tear welling in my eye, as I pushed it into my jacket pocket. My thoughts returned to the corner.

I lifted the torch. Paused. Clenched my free hand. Whispered a prayer. *Come on, James. Move. I t*ook one another, deep breath, and swung the light to the corner. To the tiny pile of bones.

An hour later, I took Mary's hand as she hopped lightly off the ladder.

"Wow!" Her eyes wide, the grin infectious.

My lips curled in a half-smile of my own. "Pretty amazing, huh?"

Candles now burned around the room, forcing the darkness to seethe in corners. The room belonged to the dark and I was a trespasser. A candle occasionally stuttered and dark shadows clawed their way back, only to be pushed away as the flame righted itself.

"You worked fast, James."

She had no idea. The candles, the swept floor, the air-freshener to cover the smell. The work of a few frantic minutes. The bones had taken most of my time. The tiny bones.

"You've built something in the corner." My heart jumped. I hoped it was enough. "A little box?" She looked puzzled.

"There was something... bad there, Mary. I think – I'm not sure, but I think a sewage pipe must be leaking or something. You really didn't want to see it. Gross."

I avoided her eyes, like a guilty husband after claiming he was working late at the office.

"How noble of you," said Mary, pecking me on the cheek. "Where's my James gone?" She turned her attention to the darkness. "I know what you're up to, hole! You've swapped my husband with a doppelgänger." She looked at me. "Well, you can keep him. I like this one better."

Mary seemed to take more pleasure in the old tins with their perfectly preserved labels than she did in the shelter itself. We discussed how we might use it. It might be a good storage room. Mary suggested growing mushrooms.

"Is it even safe?" she asked.

I looked up at the thick beams supporting the ceiling. No doubt they were also riddled with woodworm.

"I doubt it. But I could probably add extra supports." I took her hand. "We need to hold on to the past, don't you think?"

Mary held my gaze. "We're still talking about the shelter, right?" Her tone was firm.

"Of course. What else would it be about?"

"Don't be an idiot, James."

She turned, started ascending the ladder. I stood and watched her go, saying nothing.

But she hadn't quite finished

"You've got to bloody talk about it sometime!" she shouted from outside the hatch.

I stood in the pale yellow light of the candles, alone with my thoughts. Thoughts which were, and always had been mine. I realised I was holding the bear and held its rotten face up to the light. One of its glass eyes hung by a

Shelter

loose thread and the other was cracked. One of its ears was gone, whether rotten away or torn off, I had no idea. It was an ugly thing now, but he must have loved it once. The boy in the corner.

I shoved the bear back into my pocket and carefully removed the rickety wooden box I had constructed over the bones. I hadn't wanted to move them. It would be desecration. It would disturb his rest.

It didn't take a crime scene investigator to work out that the boy had died sitting against the wall, right here in the corner. The bones looked undamaged. Somehow this boy had ended up being locked in here, all alone. He had starved and died right here.

A salty tear trickled down my cheek.

"I'm sorry."

The bones didn't respond.

***

Mary put my dinner on the table and took hers back into the kitchen. She wasn't speaking to me. I guessed she was waiting for me to do something. To make some move. But I didn't know what it was. I'd tried saying sorry, but that had only brought a flash of anger to her eyes.

I picked at my spaghetti, thoughts of dead children swimming in my mind. Why had he died? It wasn't right. It wasn't fair. Someone should have done something.

"It wasn't your fault."

Mary was standing in the doorway, watching me. Desperate to escape her steady gaze, I put a mouthful of spaghetti into my mouth and chewed. All I could taste was garlic.

She released a loud, pointed sigh from the doorway.

"You know what Dave Shreeves said."

I looked up, ready to respond. To throw a few home truths back at her, but Mary had already left the room.

***

"You need to face what happened."

David Shreeves was a short man with larger than life hair and an old fashioned pair of spectacles perched on his hooked nose. He had a little clipboard and wrote things down when I spoke.

"Look, Mr Shreeves..."

"Dave, please."

"Look, *Dave*, I'm fine. It's my wife I'm worried about, okay?"

Dave looked at me over the top of his spectacles. A look I remember my mother using when I claimed it was my brother who broke her favourite vase.

"James, please. Your wife is having counselling and doing very well. She will, in time, recover." He paused, held my stare. "I am not saying she will forget, or that she will ever stop grieving, but she will be able to carry on with her life. What other choice does she have?"

I wanted to say that she had plenty of choices. The same choices I often thought about. The same choice that had led me to climb the bridge railings the previous evening. Instead, I looked down and said nothing.

"James, she wasn't there. All she has is loss. You can overcome loss. Holes can be filled in. But you *were* there, weren't you? You were there when George died."

***

The spaghetti, plate and all, smashed into the wall, leaving a red, greasy stain on the new wallpaper. I stepped into the night, slamming the door behind me.

Tears streamed down my cheeks and my eyes burned. I could see his face, George's face, the moment before the car hit. He was laughing, racing along on his little scooter. I'd called out: stop! I'd tried to grab him before he shot off the kerb. Too late. If only I had stopped him. My beautiful George.

"Daddy!" At first, I thought the voice was part of the memory, returning after two years of holding it back. But it sounded so real, like the frightened call of a lost son. "Daddy!"

The sound came from the shelter.

I froze. Trapped between memory and madness. I could see his crumpled form on the road. "Daddy, don't leave." The ambulance crew shepherded me away, his favourite, blood-splattered Winnie the Pooh hanging limply at my side.

Forcing myself out of the fog of despair, I lurched to the hatch. I could hear crying coming from inside. Harsh screams of pain and fear. Had someone fallen into the hole? I cursed myself for leaving it open. One of the neighbours kids might have climbed the hedge to get a ball. It would be my fault. Again.

Under the darkening evening sky, the hole again looked solid. I looked for the torch but I'd left it indoors.

"Daddy!"

There was no time to go back. I had to get down there. He needed me. George needed me.

I clambered onto the ladder and slid down into the darkness.

The sound of snuffling and tears grew louder as I descended. It was even colder down here than I remembered, and the smell of rot and decay was thick in the air. The candles which I had spent so long lighting had all gone out and it was pitch black. Outside, I heard Mary's voice calling, as if from a very great distance.

"George?" I whispered into the dark.

Again the same cry, "daddy!", from the darkness. I crept forward, banging my head on one of the low beams, and got down on my knees. The ground was damp with a rich, earthy smell.

I put my hand on something soft and squishy. Something furry. The bear? Blind, I ran my hands over it, recognising the shape of the eyes. The eye that had been drooping off seemed to have been fixed.

Outside, someone let off a firework. I heard a whizzing and a loud bang. The earth shook slightly. Then another whizzing sound. Another explosion. Someone's birthday, perhaps?

"Daddy, I'm scared!" The voice was tiny as bones.

"I'm here."

I crawled forward quickly and bumped into something hard. The table. A plate dropped off it and clattered to the ground. Something hard rolled against my hand.

I picked it up. A candle. One of mine? I didn't remember putting any on the table. I felt in my pockets for my lighter. It wasn't there.

"Daddy!"

I put the candle aside and crawled towards the corner. My eyes were adjusting to the light and I could make something out over there. A tiny shape.

The boy was slumped in the corner, shaking. I took off my jacket and wrapped it around his shoulders.

"I'm cold, Daddy."

"I know but I'm here now. You're safe."

He threw himself into my arms and I held him. The sounds of explosions filled the air and the ground shook. Dust fell into our hair.

"Will it ever stop?"

I didn't know what he meant but I nodded in the dark. "Yes, George, it will stop. It will all stop."

"You won't leave me, will you, Daddy?"

Explosions boomed in the night. More dust. A tinnitus whistle started in my ear. I could feel the boy shaking in my arms as he clung to me, his fingers digging into my arm.

The dark grew stronger. I gave him the little teddy bear and he settled into my arms.

Outside, between the explosions, I thought I faintly heard a voice. A woman, calling. I started to rise. It was so familiar. The boy screamed. His fingers dug into my arms. He felt heavier than the tiny child he appeared.

"Please don't leave. Please, Daddy."

Broken promises. A father's duty. I couldn't fail him again.

I closed my eyes and held him tight.

"Never."

***

Mary Jones waited up all night but her husband never returned. He'd never done this before. Never stayed out all night. Her mind kept going over the day she'd talked him down from jumping off the bridge. "I need you," she'd told him. She needed him now.

She was giving a statement to the police when she remembered the shelter. Between sobs, she managed to convince one of the officers to go down there with her. Just to check. She couldn't face it on her own. What if...

After fetching a surprisingly small flashlight from his boot, the officer opened the hatch and climbed down the ladder. Mary followed close behind. The officer flicked on the torch and the shelter burst into light. Mary's vision exploded from black nothing to white nothing.

"It's a Klarus," he said, as if this explained everything. "Sorry if it's a bit bright."

"James?" Mary whispered.

No response.

The room came into. James wasn't here. The same room. The same table. The large support beams across the ceiling. That box in the corner.

"Doesn't look like he's here, miss."

The officer turned to leave.

"Wait! Please, can you-- I want to know what's under that box."

The officer smiled and patted her on the shoulder. Why not?

He lifted the box.

Mary's head drained of blood. She sagged, faint, to the floor.

Bones.

Lots of human bones.

"James?" She whispered, tears once again pouring down here cheeks.

The officer looked at her. *Poor thing. Worry drives women in strange directions.*

"Don't worry dear. These bones are old. Probably from the war." He looked at the two skeletons again. "Quite poignant really. Father and son dying together like that."

Mary stared at the two skeletons, open-mouthed. There was something about them. Something familiar. Something nestled among the bones. Small. Splattered in blood. A teddy in a red coat. She picked it up, turned wide-eyed to the police officer and screamed.

Whitechapel

Monica Cook

Attendee: Melbourne Muggles - Melbourne, Australia

Darkness swept through the cobbled streets of East London like a ghost, devouring any lingering daylight in the habitat of prostitutes and criminals. All manner of immoral creatures lurked in the dank labyrinth of streets—searching for a place to sleep, to drink, to piss, or to fuck.

The glass fogged with his hot breath as the man stood at the window of a second floor apartment. He gazed down on the street, observing the cretins of Whitechapel. The room was stifling, and the sour smell of blood wafted through the air. The only furniture, a decaying four-poster bed, overpowered the space, filling the room with its putrid perfume.

The man pushed himself away from the window, moving languidly to the other side of the room where a black bag lay on the floor. The metallic click of the bag closure broke the dead silence of the apartment

***

The dosshouse manager threw Polly Nicholls out on the street.

"Don't yew come back 'ere until yew 'ave me faaahr pennies! I ain' runnin' a bleedin' charity!"

"Don't worry yaaahr greasy 'ead abaaaht i' Mon'ey!" Polly replied as she pointed clumsily to her head. "Look wat a jolly bonnet I got!"

With a groan, Polly pushed herself up off the frigid ground and took off her jolly bonnet. It was the colour of jaundiced skin, adorned with torn lace and greasy fingerprints. It passed inspection and she jerked it down onto her filthy, matted hair. She lurched drunkenly through the back alleys of Whitechapel searching for prospective customers.

"Good evening," an ebony voice echoed from the shadows.

Polly blinked, trying to lift the haze of drink and night.

"'Ello, darlin'." She stumbled towards the voice, but a white, gloved hand stopped her.

"Aww... come on now... 'ole Polly'll take care o' ya..." She took a step closer and eyed the tall silhouette.

"I bet yew could make Big Ben jealous!" A cackling laugh escaped her near toothless mouth and her fat body wobbled with mirth.

He could smell gin when she laughed; gin mixed with the stench of sex and dried sweat. His stomach turned with revulsion, even while his loins ached with desire. He closed his eyes for a moment, and then she was on top of him. Her scabby hands reaching out, touching him: his chest, his stomach, his groin. He looked down, but darkness swallowed all but the yellow bonnet that was bobbing up and down.

She's perfect, the voice assured him. *Take her... Now!*

A surge of anger and excitement ruptured inside of him and he lashed out.

Polly's flabby body flew through the air and crashed to the ground. Her forehead hit the brick of the building causing blood to trickle down between her eyes. Her stubby fingers splayed across her face as she clumsily removed the bonnet from her head.

"Wat da 'ell is wrong wit yew, mister?!" She screeched and held up a red hand.

Whitechapel

"Come with me " the man ordered, walking away without turning to see if she would comply.

He led Polly down the winding streets, turning frequently into dimly lit alleyways. The blackness became thicker, palpable as they moved further into the heart of Whitechapel. Polly's head throbbed as she stumbled along, trying to keep up with the billowing cape and swaying leather bag in front of her.

"Mister, I got ta stop. Please—I got ta stop..." Polly gasped for breath as she leaned up against the wall of a shabby lean-to.

The man grabbed her, his long fingers wrapping around her throat. She tried to resist, but he was too strong. The man jerked her back and forth, her head nodding falsely on her thick neck. He could feel the familiar power throbbing inside of him. In what seemed like only a heartbeat, her body went limp.

That was exquisite, the voice moaned.

The man nodded as he tenderly laid the body on the ground and unzipped his bag. Inside was an oak box inlaid with ebony and brass. He opened the latch and removed two silver knives with reverence. Kneeling down, he positioned the first blade against the throat under the left ear. He slid the metal across the soft skin, and dark blood poured onto the street of Buck's Row. He positioned the second blade and cut in the opposite direction from under the right ear.

Careful... the voice warned as the puddle of blood grew and nearly reached the man's shoes.

The man stepped away from the puddle. He knelt down on the other side of the body and slowly, laboriously inserted the tip the first knife into the belly. He pushed down, grimacing at the sound of splitting flesh and organs. He pulled the knife upward, cutting through the stomach muscles and spilling the entrails onto the street. Blood flowed from the wounds, staining the body's neck and breasts. The shadowy pools swelled beneath Polly Nicholl's body, her jolly bonnet forgotten in the ebbing tide.

***

That was wonderful work; the voice whispered.

The man nodded in silent agreement. The waiting had been worth it; the practice on the disgusting animals had been worth it. He sat on the edge of the four-poster bed and removed the scarlet coloured knives from the box. He caressed them lovingly before submerging each into a bucket. He watched, hypnotised as swirls of ruby blood cavorted in the murky water.

***

"EXTRA! EXTRA! GRUESOME MURDER! READ IT IN 'THE STAR'!"

The man stopped midstride, his long cape whirling behind him as he turned towards the paperboy.

"Give me one of those," he snapped at the street urchin. He paid for the paper and moved towards an empty alley for privacy.

MURDER IN WHITECHAPEL was written boldly across the front page.

"The throat is cut in two gashes, the instrument having been a sharp one, but used in a ferocious and reckless way. There is a gash under the left ear, reaching nearly to the centre of the throat. Along half its length, however, it is accompanied by another one which reaches around under the other ear, making a wide and horrible hole, and nearly severing the head from the body. The ghastliness of his cut, however, pales into

Whitechapel

insignificance alongside the other. No murder was ever more ferociously and more brutally done. The knife, which must have been a large and sharp one, was jabbed into the deceased at the lower part of the abdomen, and then drawn upwards, not once but twice. The first cut veered to the right, slitting up the groin, and passing over the left hip, but the second cut went straight upward, along the centre of the body, and reaching to the breast-bone. Such horrible work could only be the deed of a maniac."

"The deed of a maniac," he read aloud.

A shrill, mirthless laugh startled the paperboy who turned mid-call to stare towards the alleyway

***

Eight nights passed. The man sat at the window of the fetid apartment watching and waiting. A dark haired prostitute passed by his window each night, and he watched as she strolled with her customers. And he waited.

Tonight, my dear, the voice whispered as the man grabbed his bag and cape.

***

Dark Annie Chapman stumbled down the streets of Whitechapel.

"Bloody arse'ole. I'll get yaahar money, yew bastard," she muttered to herself then doubled over hacking, blood dripping from her lips.

"May I assist?"

Annie straightened up quickly, looking for the voice. She spotted a lean man hiding in the shadow.

"'I'm fine, love... jus' fine." She replied, her voice trembling.

The man smiled, white teeth cutting through the

darkness.

In two strides of his long legs, he was on top of her, grabbing Annie by the hair and catching her screams with his other hand. Her legs flailed as he carried her backwards through the alleyways to Hanbury Street. She was dead by the time they reached the small yard behind number 29, her swollen tongue protruding from her chapped lips.

He placed the body protectively on the ground and began the ritual: opening the bag, the box, taking out the knives. One in each hand, he trembled as he placed the cold steel against the creamy flesh of the neck. He shuddered at the fiery fervour that coursed through his veins. His broad shoulders jerked, and he prematurely slashed upwards.

What are you doing, you fool?! The voice screeched.

"I'm sorry... I..." he stuttered in shock.

He had nearly severed the head from the bloated body. He searched in his jacket for his handkerchief and tied it around the neck, trying to re-attach the skull. Thick blood instantly soaked the cloth, but it concealed the hasty misstep.

Satisfied, he ripped through the tattered dress and inserted a blade into the abdomen. This time he enjoyed the feel of the flesh and muscle resisting the momentum of the knife.

He made a large incision and pulled the gaping skin apart to search inside the cavity. He pushed slimy entrails and oozing organs aside until he found what he was looking for: the womb. Holding it delicately in one hand, he severed the attached ovaries and muscle until the uterus was free. He had to search a while longer for the kidney, but eventually found it and cut it out. With supreme care, he wrapped the prizes in a cloth and placed them in his bag. With a sense of completion, he let the surging passion envelope him and finish Dark Annie Chapman.

***

You nearly ruined it all...

The man huffed, hovering over a liquid filled jar on the bedside table. He tenderly removed the organs from the bag and slipped them into the preserve.

"Everything is fine. Everything is wonderful, in fact," he assured the voice.

Since the article in "The Star", the man collected all of the newspaper pieces concerning their work. The murder of Dark Annie was reported first in the "Lancet". The man read and reread the story with rapture. They had given him a name: *Jack the Ripper*. He delighted in the attention with a mixture of childish excitement and pride.

He continued his vigils through the silent nights. The memory of his work sustained him, and the voice drove him forward. It took nearly three weeks to spot the next woman. She was blonde and slim, so unlike the last yet every bit as unfortunate. He watched her slither by with seedy men and sulk when there were none to be found.

The first night he saw her; the man fished the kidney out of the jar. He crumpled up his nose in distaste as the acidic smell of the liquid assaulted his nostrils.

You know what we must do... the voice whispered.

Using a scalpel, he dissected the greying organ. He placed half on a white handkerchief in a silver box he had been saving for this very occasion. The other half, he fried and ate.

***

Chief Inspector Frederick Abberline sat at his desk in

the filtered sunlight of his office at Scotland Yard. He reclined back in his chair and stared at the pictures on the wall. Pictures of the Ripper victims: Polly Nicholls, Annie Chapman, and now the double-murder of Elizabeth Stride and Catherine Eddowes. The photos lost shape and detail as Abberline's eyes slipped in and out of focus.

"What makes a man like Jack the Ripper?" Abberline asked.

"You say summin', sir?" came a voice from the doorway.

Before he could answer, the two were distracted by a whirlwind of motion. A large man burst through the door.

"Blimey! I need ta see tha Inspector!" he bellowed.

The man did not wait for an answer but rushed straight into Abberline's office. He slammed a silver box down on the oak desk, ignoring the folders and paper that flew to the floor.

"What is this?" Abberline asked with feigned interest and furrowed eyebrows.

The man opened the box and slid it across the desk to rest in front of the Inspector. A greyish mass on a white handkerchief lay in the small silver coffin. The man thrust a letter in front of Abberline's face.

"It's from *'im*, Inspector!" the man responded, trembling with excitement.

From hell
Mr Lusk
Sir I send you half the Kidne I took from one woman prasarved it for you, tother piece I fried and ate it was very nice. I may send you the bloody knif that took it out

if you only wate a whil longer
Signed Catch me when you can
Mr Lusk

Abberline raised his eyes from the letter, taking in the man. He was small and fat with round, scratched spectacles and a dishevelled blue suit.
"And you would be Mr. Lusk?" Abberline enquired.
"No, sir! Mr Lusk is tha Chairman ov tha Whitechapel Vigilance Committee, sir. He delivered this to ma surgery. My name is Dr Horrocks Oppenshaw."
"Nice to meet you, Doctor..." Abberline said with a slight incline of his head. "Welcome to Hell."

***

Several murderless days passed after the double-murder of Elizabeth Stride and Catherine Eddowes. Abberline waded through the piles of letters that arrived daily at Scotland Yard. Most were hate mail. Some were rhymes or jokes, but Abberline found no humour in them. Abberline found no humour in anything anymore.

He threw down a scathing rhyme about police incompetence and leaned forward, resting his head in his hands. He had not slept since the latest murders. The pictures of the broken bodies haunted his dreams. Even daylight offered no comfort as bloody caricatures danced on the back of his eyelids.

"Are yew okay, sir?" The young constable asked.
Abberline did not trust himself to answer.
Several more days passed in a haze of floating paper and false witnesses. One witness claimed to have seen a well-dressed man in the Whitechapel area with light coloured hair and a small moustache. Another saw a man with black hair and a large curled moustache. Abberline

faced an abundance of clues, but no leads.

Police scoured the streets of Whitechapel. They interrogated butchers, Jews, doctors, prostitutes: Anyone and everyone.

"Sorry, sir. No one seems ter know anythin'." The young constable's defeated eyes reflected Abberline's withered face.

"Keep looking." The inspector ordered.

Abberline sat down on the curb of Mitre St., barely taking in his surroundings. The gargoyles from the surrounding building looked down on him with accusing eyes. The Ripper was out there. Somewhere he was planning his next kill, watching the next woman.

"Someone has to know something…" Abberline whispered, but he was not sure he believed it himself.

***

If anyone did know anything, it was too late. Three days later, the slaughtered body of Mary Kelly was found in Miller Court. Abberline encountered the young constable as he ran out of the apartment. He bent over and spewed yellow vomit onto the pavement and Abberline's shoes. He patted the young constable on the back as he passed.

Abberline stepped through the deteriorated timber doorway and into Hell. His knees buckled. For a moment, he truly believed that he had crossed through the gates of the Underworld.

The small room was an abattoir and Mary Kelly was the hog. Black, congealed blood dripped from the walls next to where a small form lay on a decomposing single bed. The face was turned toward Abberline, begging from a tepid pool of flesh and blood. Stained blonde hair fell across her face, clumps lying on the floor.

"My God...", he whispered as he stared at the woman. At least, he supposed it was a woman. The belly was ripped open exposing organs and snaking entrails. Her genitalia had been removed, and her breasts were cut off, leaving two gaping holes that led into her emaciated chest cavity.

Abberline felt hot acid rapidly rise from his stomach and erupt into his throat. He fought the urge to run away from the nightmare, far, far, away.

***

Weeks passed, and no more bodies were discovered. The residents of Whitechapel persisted and survived in the soggy, labyrinth of the East End. The papers were reporting that the Ripper was dead, but Abberline did not, could not, believe it.

Scotland Yard still had no leads, even the flood of letters had been reduced to a trickle. The Inspectors were assigned new cases; murders were still being committed in the capital even if they were not the work of the Ripper. Several months after the discovery of Mary Kelly's body, Abberline removed the victim photos from his wall. He had no doubt that the Whitechapel murders would be the biggest case of his life; his biggest case and his biggest failure.

***

The ship swayed with the rise and fall of the ocean, up and down and side to side. The man had not been able to eat since he boarded in Southampton. The constant movement of the ship was nauseating. He threw up every few hours and could barely keep any fluids inside him.

This is what we must endure to continue with our work... the voice assured him.

He knew it to be true. He had watched the

investigators from Scotland Yard scurrying around the East End like mice in a maze. Once he was even audacious enough to be interviewed by a young constable. He swore that he had seen nothing of note, nothing that would help the police apprehend the killer. The voice had giggled the whole time. The man wanted to giggle too, but he mimicked the look of concern and fear he had seen on the other faces in the crowd.

We must evolve... the voice told him. *We must go out into the world.*

When he finally emerged from the bowels of the ship, the sun was descending below the city skyline. Rising majestically in front of him, the blue, robed symbol of his new life. He had made it. He had survived to continue his work in the New World.

Welcome to New York... Jack the Ripper, the voice purred.

Skin and Bones

Kyle Yadlosky

Attendee: E3 - Los Angeles, California

Skin and Bones

Below my penthouse window, the street stretches, black as if it were paved with garbage bags. The street lamps glow a crusty yellow, choked by smog. The homeless lie on cracked sidewalks, soaking in puddles of collected human filth. Beaten cars shine white lights like ghosts searching for home. I wonder how many ghosts play late-night riders from the trunks of these cars.

"I think she's dead," Leon says, hunched over a cow of a woman. His fingers press her throat. I hope he knows to wash his hands before he touches anything.

I drag on my cigar and breathe smog. "I know she's dead. Would I call you to help me with a healthy woman?"

Blood trickles down her forehead into her still-open eyes. It blends and mats in her hair. Her mouth hangs, tongue out, trying to eat even in death. She lies sprawled; just a sad, wasted glob of human garbage.

I turn from the window and pace to the couch. My body folds onto its cushions. I can barely sit without fidgeting, wondering what's soaking in beneath me. She ruined this couch. I stub my cigar out on its arm. A tired sigh crawls from my throat. "I would like to put on my robe and turn in for the night," I tell Leon. "Can you dispose of her?"

He nods. "Would you call me, if I couldn't?"

This city is overrun with trash. One more piece won't hurt the pile.

Her name was Cynthia. She sang opera. From a box seat, I watched her body gyrate with emotion. I heard her voice carry a melody with the doves and lower to wilting flowers. Dressed in a lacy, white corset she played the part of a perfect angel. Her golden hair curled at her hips. White wings stood from her back. She threw her arms out to the sky, and her breasts swayed as she sang.

She was thin.

I had invited my driver to fetch her to my penthouse. She tapped at the door. I pulled it open, revealing her white lace, white skin, and white wings. I swept an arm to allow my angel in.

"I'm honored that you accepted my invitation," I said, and closed the door behind her. Her eyes sprung to the chandelier and gold-colored walls. They glided across royal red curtains and down to antique rugs. "Please, take a seat. Make yourself at home."

"Thank you," she said and slid onto my French couch, handcrafted with antique gold upholstery. It's not comfortable. But it's not so much for sitting in as it for admiring.

I sat next to her, pulled an arm around her shoulders. We drank red wine that was older and wiser than either of us. We kissed. My lips pecked down her neck. My fingers groped her body. I loosened the strings on her corset, shedding her from her angel's skin. My eyes bulged—my hands shot back. I saw that a beast writhed beneath. Fat rolled out in waves of filth. I revolted from the couch immediately. A yell broke from my mouth.

Her eyes stared, wide and trembling, like I was the one who had changed. She held her costume over her body, hiding herself. She apologized, moved to leave, but that would not suit me. She lifted from the couch, and I saw that her filthy imprint marked my upholstery. Her body heat tainted my furniture. She stained my home like I had opened my door to a garbage truck.

I grabbed my fire poker and slung it from the flames, throwing sparks in the air. I roared and rushed forward. A wet pounding like breaking fruit rang out over her cry and my yell. Cynthia's arms seized as they tried to reach for me. Her body convulsed, and she clattered like boulders to the ground. The poker stuck straight through her skull. My hands gripped its handle; I grunted exertion, and my Italian shoe held her body to the floor. Her neck craned as I pulled. The poker ripped free, and her head cracked to the floor. I set the poker back in the fire.

I called Leon.

Trash piles higher every day—the streets smell like graves. Unions, strikes, damn parasites asking for more than they deserve. An equal share is the share I choose for them. Beggars cannot be choosers. Somehow these people have forgotten that rule. I intend to remind them, even if I have to sink through refuse with the rest of the world.

I am the king of trash. I bought barren lots, unusable tracts of land so far off no one would ever see them. But everyone smells them. The fart smell of sewage treatment, the scent of decay that makes a man drive that much faster to get away, it's all thanks to me. No one wants to be surrounded by filth, and they pay generously to have it taken care of. I can't stand the sight of trash, garbage, refuse. The smell of it wretches my stomach. The fact that the men I pay to haul these horrors away refuse to do their jobs pains me. But I will not meet childish demands. I am the only one who demands anything. These workers will crumble before I even begin to crack. I rise high into the fresh air, while they choke on the dirt in the streets.

I am trapped in my birdcage, though. I cannot go to dinners, parties, the opera. I walk two floors down, and the scent of a dying city shoves its fingers down my throat. I rush to the elevator to escape, and I isolate myself again. All I can do is pace and stare out my window at the steadily piling trash ruining the streets.

A rundown church stands in my view. Its white paint has peeled to yellow wood. Its windows all stand in shattered fragments; no doubt rats infest its innards. I see families stroll to that church every day with bags of trash. They heave their garbage through broken windows and leave it to pile inside. I can imagine the mountains of rotting meat and spoiled food that fill its space. I can see the swaths of flies, feel the maggots crawl. I would vomit, if I ever vomited.

Outside the church, a person stands, a woman. Others walk behind and to her sides. They clasp their hands over their mouths, even close their eyes against the smell. They hurry away. Some jog. This woman stands still, staring at my building, staring up. She has blonde hair, curling by her sides. The sun dazzles over her outfit. I recognize this woman. I'm seeing ghosts.

She would have to be dead not to smell that church.

Midnight that night, a gentle hand taps my door. Slowly it pulls me from my dreams. My eyes peel open. I sit up, listen. The taps sound again. My ears buzz. I stand and pull my robe over my arms.

The stacks of trash must have found higher ground overnight; I can smell an eyelash-thin trace of rot.

I pace to the door and stop. The sounds stand still.

Then, tap, tap, tap. I've heard that knock before. The knob chills my fingers. I pull the door open. Even in the grey hallway light, I can see the beauty of the woman standing before me. Her hair hangs in perfect waves. She smiles seduction, and her eyes radiate. She's an angel.

She's Cynthia.

"How did you..." I start to ask. She runs a slender finger over my lips.

"Hush," she breathes. "The doorman let me in." She leans, and her tongue flicks against my ear. My breath stops.

"You should be dead," I whisper. My arms wrap her body, pull her close. I can't help myself.

She grabs my head and pulls it to hers for a warm kiss. Her tongue pounds at mine, waves against the shore. My head rushes. My body weakens. "Is that something a dead woman would do?" she asks.

We kiss again. We fall onto the couch. I open her angel's skin, but this time the body beneath is an angel in itself. I run my fingers down her stomach.

She's skin and bones.

We kiss. Our lips smack. Our hands wrap behind each other's heads. "Is this what you want?" she purrs again and again. "Is this what you want? Is this what you want?"

We make love.

When I wake up, I lie alone in my bed. Rancid trash curls in the air. I gag on my tongue. Soon, I won't be safe, even in my birdcage.

Leon's body rests on the couch for only a second before he jumps from the cushions, grabbing at himself. Between his fingers he grips a fat, writhing earthworm. He grimaces. "Where did you go to track this in?" he asks, waving the worm.

"Nowhere," I seethe. "It's the goddamn trash. Worms must be crawling their way up, burrowing into the walls. Just toss it out the window."

He opens the window and slings the creature to its death. He breathes the smog and sighs relief. He turns to me. "It smells better outside."

I sit, in a chair handcrafted to match my couch, with a grimace. "Shut the goddamn window," I growl. My back aches, and my legs burn. I want to sleep.

He sucks another long, contaminated breath down and shuts the window.

"Now," I pant, rubbing my back, "are you sure Cynthia was dead when you buried her?"

He looks to me, eyebrows raised. "Yeah," he says. "I knew she was dead before she left the penthouse."

"I only ask," I start, "because she came to visit me last night." I want to light a cigar, but I'm afraid it would suffocate me.

Leon shrugs. "So, you had a dream."

"No, no, she was here," I persist. "She was changed. She was thin. We made love."

"Good for you," Leon grunts. "So, you're saying that, in the last few days, this woman rose from the dead, lost a ton of weight, returned to her attacker's home, and had sex with him? It sounds like a wet dream."

I huff and shake my head. "She said the doorman let her in," I go on. "Someone else saw her."

Leon's eyebrows pull together. He steps forward. "Last night?" he asks.

I raise my voice. "Yes, last night."

"Your doorman died last night," Leon tells me. "Heart attack right at the door." He walks a circle on my antique rug, rubbing the back of his neck. "Look, you probably just heard someone talking about it before you went to bed and put together this whole thing in your sleep. It's nothing to worry about." He looks to me to see if I believe him. "Trust me, she's dead."

Every night another doorman drops dead, and every night my lover visits my bed. Every night her hair shines more and her eyes radiate deeper. She becomes more the angel she wears on her back. She's thinner, each night. My fingers run along her ribs and cheek bones. When we make love, I feel her spine pulse beneath my palms. When we finish, she rolls away, and I feel so weak I fall straight to sleep.

***

"Did you have a friendship with any of them? Is there anything you remember, however small, that could possibly help lead us to figure out why all your doormen are dying?" one of two detectives asks. We sip coffee. I slump into the couch. They stand. A fly crawls over my cheek, like a cat circling where it's going to sleep. My arm can't work the strength to slap it away. I need a cane to walk. My breath sucks down in labored pieces. It's all this trash slowly killing me.

"I don't keep relationships with doormen," I scoff. "If anything it's the trash, crawling with goddamn insects. They've probably contaminated the whole damn building."

"We're looking into that, sir," one officer assures me.

"Yes. Well, that's all I have to say." I flick my hand toward the door. "You can show yourselves out."

The officers set their coffee on the table and turn for the door. One curls his nose, then, and says, "It smells like something died in here."

***

I no longer have to peer out my window to see the diseased streets. They infest my perfect penthouse. The walls have crusted to brown. My paintings sit tarnished under layers of mud and dirt. The air hangs thick with decay. I apologize to Cynthia for the smell, and she says, "I don't smell anything."

We share a single kiss, and it steals my strength. "I don't think I have the energy to make love," I pant.

She breathes a laugh down my throat. She kisses my lips. She kisses down my neck. "If you didn't have the strength to make love," she says, "you'd be dead."

In the morning, I feel like the dead. I trod through my penthouse. Mold grows over my robe. My weak feet pat through puddles of cold mud. In the bathroom I stare in the mirror, feeling my face. I used to be fit. My chest was thick. My arms were round. Now, I have nothing.

I'm skin and bones.

At dusk, Leon drives me to the landfill. "She's out here," he says. "I know I buried her." He glances through the rear-view at my sunken eyes, and he frowns. "You look like I might have to bury you."

"I'm fine," I mutter. "Just show me this corpse."

"It's that penthouse," he goes on, pointing a finger toward his empty passenger's seat. "That place is a swamp. It'll kill you."

"It's the goddamn trash," I growl. Out the window, black bags of refuse line the sidewalks like body bags. The homeless sleep with these sacks of death. I shudder and cough into my hand.

We pull down a winding road and into the landfill.

"I can't believe we're going out to dig up the corpse of a woman you killed," Leon complains. "If anyone sees this, you take the blame. I'm feigning ignorance."

"No one will see us," I assure him.

My legs shiver with each step, dragging me to her grave. A shovel leans over Leon's shoulder. He stops suddenly, stands rigid. "God," he breathes.

"What?" I clear my throat and try to pull myself faster. I cross his side and see for myself.

The grave sits overturned; the dirt piled on either side. Leon takes slow steps to the grave's edge and peers in. He sighs relief. "She's still here, and she's still dead."

I pull my bones to the hole and look in. I see her body, brown with dirt, black with mud, crawling with worms and larva. Her eyes still stand open, mouth hanging in horror. "No," I breathe. I look to Leon. My eyes dash between him and the corpse. "I-I made love to this woman."

Leon shrugs and pulls a shovel-full of dirt. "If you did," he says, "then you made love to a corpse."

***

Midnight rolls by, and the tapping rises against my door. I'm already standing in front of it, hand clasping the doorknob. This woman is not dead. I open the door. Cynthia kisses me. She takes my hands, wrapping her fingers around mine. "Come," she says. "It's time."

"Time? What time?" I ask. She leads me from my penthouse. My legs won't turn away. I don't have the strength to control them.

Cynthia smiles, and I see a flash of broken, brown teeth. "It's the last time you'll ever make love," she purrs.

The elevator opens on the lobby. A doorman lies dead at his post. His hand claws outstretched before him. His face pulls open to terrified teeth. His eyes stare solid from their sockets. Cynthia guides me hand-in-hand over his body, through the door, and across the street to the rotten and ruined church.

"No," I argue. I try to pull my arms from hers. They refuse to fight. "I-I can't go in there!" I shout. I pull but can't break her grasp. I should be able to fight her. I killed her.

"It's the last place you'll ever go," she says.

She drags me along as I pull and yell. I can't escape. I can't break free of her. I've become an old man. What has she done to me?

We cross from the streets and into the dripping mildew of the church.

I cry out. Flies congeal to the walls and ceiling, a buzzing black mass. Larva carpet the floor. Their bodies crunch and guts squirt under our footsteps. Cynthia leads me to the front pew. "Lay down," she orders.

"No," I pant.

She throws me down. My wrist cracks. I scream. I cry. I beg in wordless tones. She runs a finger across my lips.

"Hush," she says. "This is the end."

She straddles my body. I stare, breath shuddering from my throat. Lightning flashes outside. Rain hammers the church. It seeps through and pours over us. Lightning flashes again, and my angel is gone. A corpse sprouting with torn, brown angel's wings replaces her. She rides my body. I scream out. But I can't stop. I can't fight.

My blood drains. My bones creak. My throat constricts. I hack and gurgle on my tongue. Her hands crawl with insects, holding my chest as she pumps and pounds. My head convulses, slamming into the splinters that stick from the rotten pew.

Eyes staring to the ceiling, Cynthia sings. It's a high

note that breaks over the wind and the rain. It could reach Heaven. Lightning flashes, and that note cracks and sheers to a screech. It pierces, boring into my ears like needles. Blood rolls down my ear lobes and across my neck.

My head slams back once more, and a jagged splinter spears through my skull. The church rumbles under me, but I lie still. Cynthia collapses over me. Through the shattered windows, I see the white glow of the sun beginning to rise. I pant final, deep, and laboring breaths. The air is thick with death, contagion, rot, and disease. But I can't smell anything.

Through the holes of the church, I peer up to my shuttered penthouse window. I would reach for it, if I could move my arms. I am no longer a bird in a cage. I'm just more filth on the street. My throat rattles. My eyes close.

This city is overrun with trash. One more piece won't hurt the pile.

Red Cove

Michael Mohr

Attendee: SF Writer's Conference - San Francisco, California

I see why they call this bar a cove: Dim red light glows; it closes in and permeates the walls—it's inside of me and John.

Bikers, aging muscle-men with ponytails and leather jackets, slump on their bar stools, or on their women.

John muffles a cough followed by a burp. I wink at him, swerving my head and smiling. I still can't believe he fucked Gloria last week—she's the only girl I've ever been loyal to. But John and I'd grown up together; he was like surrogate family, plus the only guy in town who kept up with my drinking. I had to pretend to forgive him. For now at least.

"Ahhh don' worry buddy, we're fine. Ain't *nobody* gonna' do nuthin', man. C'mon," I say.

He looks around. Black eyes search for an answer to my bravado. His energy almost carries a vestige of an apology.

My mind isn't on leaving—it's on women. I scan the place. They're everywhere, mostly older, mostly taken, the taken ones wearing their men's leather jackets.

I zero in on one.

She's standing alone under the bright light of the pool table, practically begging someone to come over and talk. Hell's Angels all around, but none talk to her or even pay attention. I slug what's left of my beer and slump up to Johnny, the bartender, and order another. I toss back half of the second pint and slam the glass.

"John, my man, I'm gonna go talk to that broad.

That's right, I'm gonna nail that bitch."

John looks at me, and his eyes comprehend. The vestige has disappeared.

"Man, you go over there—it's all over. You hear me man? All over. There's more Angels here than lights on a Christmas tree."

I gulp the rest of my beer and hammer the table. John reaches for my arm, but I fling him off, plant one foot in front of the other across the room. Up the two steps to the pool table, the light brightens; a new white aura surrounds me, replacing the red, resonant glow. She catches me out of the corner of her eye.

We're locked in.

She nudges her nose with her finger. Something is wrong.

"You're beautiful honey," I say. I should feel more confident.

Her pupils magnify into cannons, then retreat back to pin points. I notice, close-up, wrinkles on her face and bad make-up. A sharp pulse rips through my spine at terrifying speed. The mixture of harsh light in the room and her stare throw me off balance.

Something is definitely wrong.

"Look darlin', I 'preciate you sayin' that an' all—but I'll say—you better get going becau—"

A huge hand clutches my shoulder.

I shudder—turn—expecting to get plowed in the face with such force that death would feel better. It doesn't happen.

His face is mean; blue eyes blaze, his face wide, cheeks far apart, separate, as if they had been ripped apart at birth and stitched together afterward. Six-foot-five, 280, bulging out of his leather jacket: *"Hell's*

Angels California."
"*Hey you sonofabitch*! That's my wife, motherfucker. You better 'ave a damn good excuse fer botherin' 'er, kid."
Everyone is suddenly still. The whole bar watches. Still at the booth in the corner, John sits paralyzed, a drunken gleam in his eyes, his two-toned hair disheveled, mouth open, face transfixed. *Gloria...*
"Well boy, what the hell ya have ta say fer yerself, huh?"
"Wait," the woman interrupts. "He didn't mean no harm, Bill. I think he's just drunk... he's just a fuckin' kid anyhow, barely old enough ta' drink... what're you...twenty-one?"
I gulp and look at Bill. I notice for the first time a pool cue in his hand, balanced in the air. A patron coughs. I startle. Angels hold their positions. The woman stands motionless.
"Shit," I say. "I'm sorry. I didn' realize what I was doin... I just didn' know. I'm kinda loaded—"
"*Johnny, close the door.*"
Bill stares straight at me.
Johnny knocks the deadbolt home. He returns to behind the bar. All eyes are back on Bill. Out of nowhere Bill smashes the cue stick in half on the pool table—a deafening sound—still holding the bottom portion, splinters projecting.
"*Bill*—" the woman starts.
"Now listen boy, you and yer faggot friend go stand in the middle of the room."
I stagger and motion John. We stand. My heart is beating like a silent machine gun. Angels walk over, forming a semi-circle around us, barring the doorway, as

if the dead bolt weren't enough.

"*Look, you little maggot-piece of shit*. I could beat you so bloody you'd never walk again. I could kill you. Shit, I can do whatever I want man, *I'm a god-damn Hell's Angel, fer Christ sakes*! Nobody fucks with an Angel, you got that, motherfucker!"

I nod. Life is precious.

"...*Nobody*, you stupid sonofabitch. Tonight's yer lucky night. I'm gonna let you and yer queer friend go. That's right. But don't ever come back to The Red Cove; ya hear me boys? Never! I hear 'bout you comin in an' real shit's gonna happen...you won't like it. Am I making this clear, boy?"

"Yes sir."

Bill looks at all the Angels, then at Johnny. Johnny hurls himself over the bar and unlocks the door, throwing the dead bolt back. The red door peels in the light outside. I smell filthy, broken-in leather as we tremble past each Angel.

Bill comes out behind us, arms at his waist, then gives us a shove.

"All right faggots, hit it... get the hell outta here!"

John and I collide, trip on ourselves before getting our balance. We begin hobbling up the street. That's when I hear it—hear the thing cock—an obscure click. I look back.

Bill holds a gun.

He points it at us.

"*I said run you filthy maggots, RUN*!!!"

We start running, almost colliding again, but this time running fast, fast as we can, swerving all over the road. We're on a residential street, the edge of a suburban tract.

I hear the first shot—see movement in the brush to my right.

We run faster. Shots continue, each one seeming louder, louder, louder. I put my hands to my ears, sweating. I sprint past John, breathing hard, panting, spitting bits of bile from my stomach. John's slowing. I keep running.

Another shot.

Somehow I increase my speed a notch.

I feel the curve of the street and try to bend with it. Hitting a bump and crashing, my palms slide out, skin on asphalt, my head hits the ground; blood everywhere, jeans ripped, skin raw, dirt and rocks in my mouth. Get back up: adrenaline pumping. *Where is John?*

I hit Ocean Avenue, hook a left until I reach 1678: *Jimmy's house.* It's almost 2 A.M., but Jimmy's light shines. I run up to the door, fall on it, pounding. I hear yelling, moving. Jimmy comes to the door, pissed.

"What in the name of fuckin...Jesus H. Christ, what happened dude?"

"Lemme' in man, shit! I need...jus' fuckin' lemme in dude!"

I head for the bathroom. Jimmy follows, sees my wounds in the light.

"Holy shit man, you need medical assistance," Jimmy says.

"Can't afford that shit, ya bastard."

"At least let me bandage you up. We have gauze and medical tape in here, lemme look."

Jimmy orders me to shower, bandages me up. He says I'm damn lucky to be alive and makes up the spare room, pulling the bed out and putting sheets on.

He and his girlfriend go back to whatever it was they

had been doing before I showed. Probably screwing. The lucky bastard. I wish that's what I had been doing, instead of running from the god-damn Hell's Angels.

Turning off the light and crawling into bed, I try to get comfortable but my body hurts. Two windows are open, and the moon hovers above palm trees. Glancing at the phone, 911 flashes through my mind—John might be in serious trouble.

I think about dialing but remember what happened last week. If it had only been a kiss. Then it might have been forgivable. But it was more than a kiss. So, so much more.

Origins 1995

Kathleen Molyneaux

Attendee: Con on The Cob - Hudson, Ohio

Thursday, July 13th

"**K**elly, get your fat butt down here!" Chuck's voice snapped me out of my thoughts. I had been day dreaming about vampires. Last night, I'd rewatched <u>Bram Stoker's Dracula</u> explaining to Chuck that it was research for a roleplaying game I was planning. I shook my head and tried to focus more on my packing and less on fantasies about Gary Oldman. I tossed some deodorant and a hairbrush in on top of my clothes and dragged my duffle bag down the stairs.

"Great! You ready?" Chuck grabbed my duffle and headed for the door.

"Wait, Chuck. I need my dice-bag. Have you seen my dice-bag?" I sputtered.

"Oh, just buy some when you get there, Kelly." The door slammed behind him leaving me to search the living room. My dice collection was in a green leather bag with a capital "K" in gothic script embossed on one side. I had bought the bag and most of the dice at a previous gaming convention. My dice were like old friends. Some were ugly but reliable; some pretty but capricious. They needed to be taken out and shown off, and 'Origins' was the best place for it.

'Origins' or more formally the 'Origins Game Expo' was the convention to end all conventions, the big one, the big 'O'. My college friends and I had spent the past five months talking about it. We discussed the games we'd bring, the events we'd try, and the swag we'd buy. I simply had to bring my dice. It would be embarrassing to borrow someone else's. Unfortunately, thirty seconds wasn't enough time for me to spot them, and I could hear the horn of my car blaring outside.

"Kelly! Come on! We said we'd pick up Dave and Jennifer by 10." My boyfriend was so impatient sometimes. If I'd known he'd be dead in less than a week, I might have found this quality endearing. Instead, I just sighed, gave up on the dice and dashed for the door. We got to the dorms by 10:45, loaded Dave, Jennifer and their luggage into the car and were on the road.

We arrived in Philly by 5 pm, just in time for the first evening of the con. We dropped off our bags in the hotel room, registered, got our badges and went immediately to the dealer's room. Chuck wanted to be first in line for whatever new collectible card game, or "CCG" was coming out. The dealer's room was huge and already packed with people buying or selling T-shirts, dice, books, miniatures, and games, bright and shiny new games.

While I was staring at the games, Chuck and Dave stopped to stare at a few skinny chicks in costume; looked like Power Girl and Cat Woman. Jennifer frowned at Dave's obvious ogling, but I enjoyed this part of the con. Costumes were fun and there were always a few women with builds like mine strutting their stuff in spandex. I loved them. They were brave, and they highlighted the best thing about the gaming world, acceptance.

"Hey. Look at the fat chick in the Wonder Woman costume!" Chuck laughed.

So much for acceptance.

"Like you're Brad Pitt," I snapped back.

"Well...no, but at least I don't take my ugly out and wave it in everyone's face."

"She's not ugly. She's just average. I think she's brave."

"You two stop arguing, and Dave stop staring. You're all pissing me off." Jennifer grumbled.

Chuck shrugged, Dave studied the floor, and I started walking. Buying something would help me recover from the argument. I picked up some new dice made from a pretty combination of red and orange resins. I also bought a copy of "Die Siedler von Catan", a board game fresh from Europe that was rumored to have the most revolutionary game mechanic ever.

"Looks like it involves a lot of dice rolling. How revolutionary is that?" Chuck scoffed, but since he'd just picked up an entire box of Magic booster cards, he was feeling benign and agreed to give "Settlers of Catan" a try. The four of us ended up eating pizza and playing for the rest of the evening.

Friday, July 14th

The first full day of the con was miserable. Chuck's magic tournament started at 10am and I ended up stuck being the third wheel to the little love bugs. They were freshmen, and gamers to boot, so the whole relationship thing must have been pretty new to them. I was a senior and had been dating Chuck for the past two years. This meant that other people's public displays of affection tended to make me wince.

Dave, Jennifer and I played a few games, but Dave kept maneuvering so that Jennifer would win. This started to piss off the other gamers at our table. I tried to cover for Dave and Jennifer by whispering that they were in love and all, but that just turned me into the target. My game piece got shot at and shoved into pits multiple times. I came in dead last in our final RoboRally match.

Over lunch, I tried to give Dave and Jennifer some pointers on gaming etiquette, but they were too busy gazing at each other to pay attention. So that afternoon, I suggested we take a break from games and visit the dealer's room again.

The room was too crowded to be much fun. I got jostled by an Asian guy dressed up as Wolverine. His pasty faced girlfriend sneered at me over her sunglasses while the guy yelled at me. "Why don't you watch where you're walking, you fat cow." I was too rattled to sass back. Then, I got stuck downwind of some pudgy guy in a TSR t-shirt with a serious case of gamer funk. He was so rank that it made me gag. The final straw came when I ended up in line behind a tall guy in a beard and baseball cap. Mr. Grizzly Adams couldn't figure out what T-shirt he wanted to buy. After ten minutes, I gave up, left the line and told the love bugs that I was going to go see how Chuck was doing in the Magic tournament.

I bolted from the Dealer's room, but not quickly enough to outdistance the cloud of ill-will that seemed to be following me. Chuck was in the process of losing to a 14 year old in the semifinals. When I sat down at the table to watch their game, Chuck barely grunted at me and then proceeded to lose six life points to a Ball Lightning card. After that, the end came swiftly.

"You distracted me, Kelly." Chuck grumbled as he

was cleaning up his cards. "I couldn't focus with you standing behind me breathing heavy the way you do. Why don't you lose some weight?"

I hadn't been standing behind him, I hadn't been breathing heavy, and I WAS working on losing weight. It's just that traveling tended to mess with my diet.

"Where's Dave and Jennifer? Are we meeting them for dinner?" Chuck got up and started towards the door without even shaking hands with his opponent.

"Congratulations on your win and good luck in the finals," I said to the teenager. I hurried to catch up with Chuck. We found Dave and Jennifer, and finally decided on "Max and Erma's" for dinner. I ordered a salad.

Chuck spent most of dinner complaining about the kid that he'd lost to. After listening to that I decided my salad required a cheesecake chaser and maybe a visit to the ice cream sundae bar. The hell with my diet. Dave and I made a beeline for the ice cream, leaving Jennifer to listen to Chuck whine.

Losing in the semi-finals didn't keep Chuck from spending the rest of the evening playing pickup games of Magic with other players who had washed out of the official tournament. They called themselves the "losers bracket" and they were still playing at midnight. I watched for a while and then played games with Jennifer and Dave until the two of them decided to head back to our shared hotel room. They were cooing at each other so I decided to delay going to sleep for a while. Chuck was still engrossed with his cards and shrugged when I told him that I was going to take a walk.

There were only a handful of gamers left in the main hallway, and most of them were asleep on the floor. At the west end, a pair of Klingons was poking at each other with foam bat'leths, but even they looked tired. I walked down the hallway. I couldn't remember where the boardgame room was, so I stopped halfway down to check my convention booklet.

I was squinting at the map in the dim light when I heard footsteps behind me. I glanced back, but there wasn't anyone there. Even the Klingons had vanished. It was cold and dark. I dropped my map and tried the first door I came to. Big mistake. It was the dealer's room and it was closed for the night. The room was darker than the hallway and full of tables and booths covered in sheets. I thought I saw something move in there. I jumped back into the hallway and tried to retrace my steps. The card room was lit; Chuck was there. If I could convince him to stop playing for a moment, he could walk me back to the hotel. But there were footsteps behind me again and this time I was sure I saw someone. I had the impression of a tall, spindly shape, a white face, one glittering eye. I shrank against the wall and hoped that it would just walk past me. The shape dwindled as it came close and suddenly resolved into a pudgy guy wearing a dark t-shirt and jeans. He grinned at me and shrugged. "Are you planning on trying out some role-playing?"

"What?" I said. My heart rate hadn't quite returned to normal yet.

"Here, allow me." He reached around me and opened a door that I hadn't noticed. "Ta-da!" he said and flourished a hand towards the room. "That's the role playing room."

"Did you follow me from the card room?" I thought I remembered seeing someone who looked like him. He was about 5'6" and stocky. He had a round, pale face, scraggly brown hair and brown eyes. His T-shirt had a dragon logo on it, and the letters "T" "S" "R".

"Why would I do that?" He smiled again. He had a nice calming sort of smile. Of course I hadn't been followed. He was just a gamer guy, a cute one actually.

"Let's find a game to join, shall we?"

"All right," I mumbled. "I play D&D at school."

"Perfect," he said. "Table over there."

A group of three people were already at the table. There was a woman sitting behind a card board GM screen. She had short blonde hair, pale beige eyes and colorless worm-like lips. I shook my head. The fluorescent lighting in here was making everyone look a bit ill. I kept my eyes off her face and on the screen. Her two players were an Asian dude with glasses in a "Wolverine" T-shirt and a tall, bulky guy with a beard and a "Phillies" baseball hat.

The guy I met in the hallway sat down. "Hi guys, this is Kelly." I was pulling out a chair when it occurred to me that I hadn't mentioned my name. It also occurred to me that I hadn't registered for this game. "Do you need generics?" I thought I might have a few tickets left.

"Nah. It's a pick-up game for insomniacs." The GM had a surprising voice. I was expecting something dull and whispery, but she sounded like a sixteen year old cheerleader. She handed me a pre-filled character sheet. It was a Barbarian. I loved playing fighters; they were easy to understand and smashing things was cathartic.

"I'm Gina. The guy with glasses is Paul. He's playing a Ranger. The big fuzzy guy is Eric. He's playing a wizard. How 'bout you Frank? Thief or Cleric?"

"Cleric, I guess. Someone needs to patch up the inevitable trauma." Frank was looking at me when he said that. Or rather, one eye was looking at me. I hadn't noticed before, but Frank was a bit wall-eyed. His left eye would move and focus normally, while his right tended to point off into space. About a minute ago I'd thought this guy was good looking. Eww.

"How did you know my name," I whispered to Frank while Gina was launching into the story.

"Your Con badge of course. Shhh...."

Gina ran a good game. I forgot I was tired. I forgot how weird they all looked. I even stopped noticing the occasional odd smell coming off of Frank. I thought I had smelled something like it earlier today, but I couldn't remember where. It wasn't just the usual gamer funk. It was like a combination of incense and rotting meat, but even that couldn't distract me from the story.

Our party had been hired by a merchant prince. He was trading in weapons, providing pikes, swords and armor for the warring border kingdoms. Recently, several of his shipments had vanished in the mountain pass between the Southlands and the unsettled North. The only remaining survivor from the last caravan had brought back word of a dragon attack in the mountains. We were hired to protect the next caravan and to investigate the prior disappearances. Our employer suspected interference from a political rival. The attacks were too organized, and it seemed like someone knew precisely when the shipments would be sent.

We devised a plan before leaving the city with the next caravan. I found myself giving orders. "You. Ranger. Locate maps and scout the travel route. Mage, use your powers. Pry secrets out of the mind of the survivor. Cleric, mumble to your god. Tell him to give us success in battle." Frank rolled his eye at me for that.

Turns out the survivor knew that one of the prince's

seneschals was selling inventory and travel information to a rival merchant family. I got to beat the tar out of the traitor until he 'fessed up and gave us the name of his employer. He'd already passed on our current travel plans and choosing a new route would delay the sale by weeks. We decided to risk the mountain pass anyway. I stomped through snowstorms, goblins, and a dragon that turned out to be an illusion. We defeated the rival family's mage and his body guards in a blood fest of swinging swords. I think I was standing over the body of the mage roaring out some kind of battle song when Gina called it quits.

"Ummm....you can sit down Kelly. That was epic, guys. You just walked all over my NPCs, but it's 5:00 am."

I plopped back down into my seat. My face felt hot. Had I monopolized that last battle scene? Chuck always hated it when I talked too much.

"Shall we finish up tomorrow? We can pick up again at midnight. Kelly, does that work for you? You're fun, girl. We'd love to have you back."

"Wait. That wasn't the end of the story? I thought we solved it."

"Oh no, " Frank said. "Story's not over by a long shot. We think..."

Gina cleared her throat and cut him off. "You need to deliver the weapons, right? Tomorrow at midnight? More barbarian rampage."

"Definitely! I'll be here. That was a great game. Sorry if I got bossy. Goodnight everyone."

I got up and started towards the door. I couldn't believe I'd been up all night. I was exhausted but elated. The game had been wonderful. It had made me forget my miserable day; it had even made me forget about food for a couple hours.

In the hallway, I heard footsteps again then got a whiff of raw meat as Frank popped up on my right. "You don't need to bring Chuck, tomorrow."

"Why do you smell like that?" I was too tired to care if I offended him.

"Been busy playing games. Haven't bothered to shower. You know how it goes." He smirked. Frank was getting on my nerves.

"Chuck doesn't like roleplaying games; he says they're for kids. You know 'let's pretend'?"

"Well...let's pretend that he's an idiot. You can learn a lot playing any kind of game and role playing can reveal your true character. "

"At a con, you just play whatever pre-generated character they hand you. It's not deep, Frank. Frank?" He was striding down the hall and was already twenty feet away.

"Fine, be that way you freak." I muttered to myself. Get your nasty stare, your nasty smell, and your little smirk out of my face. I hope I see you tomorrow.

Saturday, July 15th

Tomorrow started at about 11 am for me. I'd been up so late that it took me forever to wake up. Chuck, Dave, and Jennifer had left a note and some bagels in the room. I chewed on a sesame bagel and considered my options for the day. Chuck had written that he was going to be in the CCG room until noon playing the newly released Illuminati card game. Card games were the last thing on my mind right now. I kept thinking about barbarians and magic users. That game last night had been amazing. Was I really going to have to wait a whole twelve hours before finishing the story?

I was still thinking about it when I met up with Chuck in the CCG room.

"Late night, Kelly?"

"I ended up in this really wonderful D&D game. It was all about weapons dealing, politics, and war. Amazing plot. We figured out that the Dunleve family was behind the raids on the weapon shipments and defeated the mage they hired to harass the caravan route. I mean we thought there were dragons initially, but...."

"Your story has grown tiresome." Chuck cut me off mid-way through.

"Ahh. OK. You were up pretty late to. How'd the Magic go?"

That was apparently the wrong question. "Well...you already know that I'm out of the tournament, right?" Chuck started complaining about unfair deck design again.

"Maybe we should both play something else this afternoon?" I suggested as soon as I could get a word in again. We agreed to try out a miniatures system, and over lunch we talked Dave and Jennifer into joining us. The game was based on the shootout at the OK Corral and used Lego minifig cowboys. The four of us were running the Earp faction while four other gamers were playing the Clantons. Historically, the shootout took 30 seconds; our Lego battle took 2 hrs. I kept overestimating my range and most of my shots were wasted. I think I clipped a cow at one point. The Clantons shot down the three Earp brothers, and Doc Holliday had to escape on horseback.

"Wow, Kelly," Chuck said. "You couldn't hit the broad side of a barn there. Why didn't you move up?"

I shrugged. "Trying to stay under cover."

"It didn't happen that way, historically," he said.

"It's a game, not a simulation, Chuck."

Jennifer jumped in at that point. "I thought it was fun, even though I got shot."

"I don't think I got enough sleep last night. Couldn't seem to keep the rules straight." I stood up, stretched and yawned. "Dinner? At the very least, I need some caffeine."

The large Coke revived me enough to watch Chuck play a few more rounds of cards that evening. I kept looking at the clock. I had another Coke.

"Chuck, I'm going to go finish up that D&D game tonight. We're starting at midnight. I don't think it'll be as long as last night."

"Yeah, yeah. Have fun." He was winning and that always made him happy.

I was half an hour early for D&D. Frank nodded at me, but the rest of the group wasn't there yet. I sat down. I played with my dice. I stood up. I walked around the table. Frank's single functioning eye tracked me.

"Wired?" He asked.

"Can't wait to get started. It's been a long day."

"Gina does know how to draw you in, doesn't she? Girl has talent."

"Do you run a game?"

"I don't run…games, at least." Frank laughed.

I laughed too even though I felt like I was missing something. Frank was weird as ever. I plopped down in my seat. "Do you think we'll get the caravan to Pine

Ridge?"

"I wouldn't count on it. Gina will up the ante. We'll probably have a total party kill tonight. We'll just have to go out with glory, right?"

"Sing your death song and die like a hero going home." I replied.

"Precisely!" Frank stood up and waved. "Hey Gina, you going to take it easy on us tonight?"

She certainly didn't. We finished escorting the caravan through the pass and were only an hour outside Pine Ridge when our Ranger spotted smoke, a lot of smoke. Pine Ridge had been torched, and most of the population turned into zombies. The fighting went on for hours. Once the last zombie had been hacked to bits, we tried to decide what to do about the caravan. Paul said that the buyers were dead and that we should just escort the shipment back through the pass.

"I want to find out who did this to Pine Ridge. But first the barbarian needs a bathroom break. Sorry guys. Too much Coke." I got up and headed for the hallway.

Like last night, the main hall was dim and nearly empty, but the echoes didn't bother me as much. I had just crushed a horde of zombies after all. I strode into the ladies room like I owned the place.

I was finishing up when I heard the door to the bathroom open. The footsteps slowed, and the light was briefly blocked as whoever it was moved past my stall. I flushed and headed for the sink, washed quickly and turned to look for a hand dryer. Frank was standing about three feet behind me. I nearly jumped out of my skin. I hadn't noticed any movement in the mirror.

"Jesus, Frank! You scared me. This is the ladies room, you pervert! The men's room is the first door..." I never finished that sentence. Frank lunged at me. My back smashed into the sink, and my head snapped back, slamming the mirror. I saw stars. Frank was holding my left shoulder and had something bright in his left hand.

'Is he acting out something from the game?' I thought inanely. Then, the bright thing flicked at my neck. "Frank? What are you doing? That hurts." I was sure I'd been shouting, but that came out more like a bubbling whisper. I was dizzy and tired. Thought I'd just lay down for a minute. It got black for a time. I heard voices.

"The rest of you, get out! I'm not done yet." It sounded like Frank, but really far away. Wish they'd all just shut up and let me sleep. "Come on, Kelly. Come on, girl. You can do it. It's not that hard. Come on back, my little barbarian." Frank just kept droning on and on. That man was irritating.

About a century later, I woke up. I was lying on a wet floor staring at the bottom of a sink. I laid there for another minute trying to piece together what had happened. Nothing hurt. I felt fine. Well, I felt sticky and I badly wanted a shower, but other than that, I was fine. I tried rolling over and spotted a pair of Converse high-top Chuck Taylors. The shoes were attached to some feet that were attached to Frank. He was leaning against the door of one of the stalls and sucking on the blade of a straight razor like the thing was a lollipop. He popped it out of his mouth long enough to say, "Welcome back."

"What?" I got to all fours and cringed away from Frank.

"Gina will be disappointed. They get to eat the ones that die for real."

"What?" I stood up.

"How do you feel?"

"What?" I felt nearly good enough to run away.

Frank stared at me with his one good eye. "Your vocabulary was more varied when you were living." He shrugged. "Maybe you're still in shock."

Some of it what he was saying was starting to sink in. "I'm dead? I don't feel dead."

"You're only kind of dead. For a while there you were completely dead. You got over it. Not everyone does."

"This has got to be some kind of bizarre gaming prank. Pig blood right?" I waved at the floor.

"You, my dear are no pig. We tested you first, and you passed. The one's that fail the test are pigs, just fodder really."

"Why are you pulling this prank on me?"

He chewed on the blade of his straight razor for a minute. "You mean, why did we recruit you? Three reasons really. You were appetizing. You stood out even amongst a throng of out of shape gamers. Your fasting blood glucose level was around 120 mg/dl, and your triglycerides were up around 300. But that just attracted us. What made you able to change, well I guess it's a particular combination of misery and savagery. You were a very good barbarian by the way." He shrugged.

"I smashed things in a roleplaying game and that enabled me to transcend death?" I wasn't afraid anymore. I was starting to feel some of that savagery coming back into play.

"Anyone can smash things. You became the role."

"So, my blood was tasty and I have an overactive imagination. That's two reasons. You said there were three?"

"Consider yourself. You're short, dumpy and unremarkable. You are my greatest work of art. A perfectly camouflaged killer." Frank giggled. "And your first job as my creation is to clean up this mess." He gestured at the streaks of blood still left on the floor.

I launched myself at him, and as predicted, he didn't see it coming. I knocked him flat on his back, and the razor skittered into one of the stalls. "I'm fucking sick of people criticizing my looks and you can clean up your own damn mess, you creep!" I had my hands around his neck and proceeded to slam his head against the floor. He was laughing and talking the entire time. "Kelly..." <whap> "I said..." <whap> "...your looks are..." <whap> "an advantage.." <whap>. On the last slam, the door of the ladies room burst open and Gina, Paul and Eric leaped into the scrum. Eric grabbed me, ripped me off of Frank and tossed me into the wall. Paul followed that up with a kick and Gina came in low with a knife.

Somehow, I was ready for it. I deflected Paul's kick with my left hand and brought my right fist down on Gina's head. That stretched her flat on the floor for a moment, but she still had the knife and was heading for my ankles. She was hissing and swearing.

I stomped on her knife and made a feint at Eric who was making another lunge. He fell for it and slammed into the wall where I'd just been standing. I leaped through the door and ran down the main hall. Behind me, I could hear Frank's nasal laugh. "When you get hungry don't hunt here, my dear. This herd is mine."

I made it to the escalator, ran down to the first floor, and streaked out to the street without getting winded. I fled towards my hotel expecting the four of them to jump out of every shadow I passed on the way. I reached my room and collapsed in bed next to Chuck. I spent the rest of the night listening for the sound of pursuit, but heard nothing but Chuck, Dave and Jennifer breathing. By 5 am, I'd relaxed and decided I'd imagined most of this.

I got up and went into the bathroom. I stripped off my stiff t-shirt and frowned at the large blood stain covering the front and left side. I sniffed it. It smelled like steak. I was starving. Barbecue would be fantastic right about now, but what barbecue place would be open in Philly at 5 am? I showered and rinsed my shirt at the same time. Despite the soap, I could still smell blood. Damn, I was hungry.

I toweled off and tried to think about something other than food. I'd always struggled with my weight and had spent much of my life on some kind of diet. This meant that I had a lot of practice feeling hungry. I could ignore this, right? But it didn't seem to make much sense anymore. I mean why did I care what I looked like? Was I doing this for Chuck? Would he suddenly become a decent person if I were thin? While I was thinking, I idly picked up one of Chuck's three-bladed safety razors and tested it with a finger. It could cut. Not deeply that was the point of a safety razor after all, but it might be good enough.

I walked back out to the bedroom with the Gillette in my hand. Just a little nick, right? It won't even wake him up. I used the razor to make three tiny slashes on Chuck's arm. He kept on snoring. I ran a finger over the scratches and licked off the blood. It was like getting a tiny hit of the best prime rib ever. Chuck mumbled something and pulled his arm back. This wasn't going to work; all I was going to get this way was a few measly drops. There had to be a quicker way to get the blood out of him, but after that, what would I do with the body? And what about Dave and Jennifer?

I glanced over at the other bed. I could kill them too, but they didn't smell nearly as appetizing as Chuck. Chuck did have a family history of cholesterol problems. That made me cringe and suddenly remember Frank's comment about glucose and triglyceride levels. "Oh God, no." I dropped the razor, pulled on a clean t-shirt and jeans and headed for the door.

Sunday, July 16th

It was daylight outside and the sun hurt my eyes. Wasn't I supposed to burst into flame? Then I thought back and remembered seeing Frank, Gina, Paul and Eric at the con during daylight hours. Gina had sunglasses at one point. I'd get some of those and a knife. Though maybe the knife could wait until I got home.

I went back to the convention center and took the escalator up. The hallway had started filling with people sharing coffee and donuts or starting card games on the floor. The Klingons were back passing out recruitment literature. I tried to walk casual, but all the gamers smelled like bacon. I managed to make it to the bathroom without killing anyone. The floor was spotless and the broken mirror had been removed. Apparently, Frank had found someone else to clean up the mess. I closed myself in a stall and leaned my head against the door. I was so hungry. How was I going to make it home like this?

The rest of the morning passed in a painful haze. I met Chuck, Dave and Jennifer outside the dealer's room. "Up all night, Kelly? Did you manage to finish that stupid game?" Chuck grinned at me. I just stared at him and swallowed. He was making me drool.

"Come on, sleepy head, wake up," he laughed. "You're going to need to drive home soon. But first guys, one last shopping trip. I have some more cards to buy."

I followed Chuck, Dave, and Jennifer into the dealer's room and stopped to stare at one of the tables selling prop swords and knives. I picked up one to test its edge. Stupid thing wasn't even sharp.

Chuck slapped me on the shoulder, "Really Kelly? Going to take up fencing?"

"Just thought it might look good on the wall," I mumbled, hurried after him, and stood there while he bought his final pack of cards.

At lunch, I wolfed down twenty chicken nuggets, a large fry and a Coke.

"Whoa...slow down there chow-zilla." Chuck grimaced.

"I need chocolate," I said around the last nugget.

"Well...we'll handle checking out. You can meet us at the car when you're done eating." He stomped off and Dave followed. Jennifer and I walked to the vending machines.

"You OK, Kelly? You look ill." Jennifer patted my arm.

I guess she'd noticed the large sweat stains streaking my shirt. This made me angry, and I nearly growled at her. I mean if I was undead, why was I still sweating? It was unfair and gross. It wasn't like the movies at all. I told her I was OK, ate a packet of M&Ms and went to find Chuck.

The drive home was hell. Everyone in the car fell

asleep except for me. Listening to them breath just made me feel even hungrier. It was starting to smell like thanksgiving dinner in here.

I don't know how I made it back to Rochester, but I did. We dropped off Dave and Jennifer at the dorms. I only needed to wait another fifteen minutes before Chuck and I were alone in our apartment. Fifteen minutes before I could grab one of the kitchen knives, kill him, drink his blood and stuff his body in the trunk of my car.

Since then, I've been on the road. Chuck's body went over the falls late at night in Niagra. I switched cars and kept driving. Near as I can tell, no one ever traced our disappearance and it's been eighteen years. Frank may still be picking off people at Origins, but I stalk the smaller local cons now, moving from Dex Con, to Tenn Con to An Con, to Glitch Con to Orc Con, and back around again. I like to think I have a code. I mostly eat the people who cheat at games, borrow other people's dice, ridicule roleplaying or break any other gaming rule I care to make up. But really, who am I kidding? Everyone I've eaten has been overweight, diabetic, and easy to run down. I can't help it. Gamers are delicious.

The Doll

Patrick Van Slyke

Attendee: Renaissance Pleasure Faire
Irwindale, California

The lightning didn't so much boom as explode, filling Steven's room with blinding light and a sound so loud that it cracked his window and threw him to the floor. When he recovered enough to pull himself upright, he looked out the window and his mouth dropped open in wonder. The old giant elm, the glory of the street and the home of his tree house, had been cloven in two and burned with a white fire, daring the rain to try to put it out. It looked like a great flaming V, almost like a gate to another world.

"Oh...my...God." Steven articulated as he automatically began to pull on his pants and shirt.

As he tied his shoes, he heard his little sister yelling from across the hall in excitement. "The tree! Mom, look!"

He smiled as he jumped up from his bed and headed out into the storm. Nothing this exciting ever happened.

"Steven!" his dad yelled. "Do not go out... "

The door slammed behind Steven before his father could finish his sentence. This was one of those once in a lifetime things. Just wait until he told the guys in school about this!

The storm seemed to have spent its fury on the strike against the tree. The wind was gone, leaving just a slight drizzle which was working on putting out the fire. The ground squished under his sneakers, and he skidded to a stop as the heat from the tree hit him. The sight was incredible. It looked as if the mighty elm had exploded from the inside out, throwing branches and large chunks of jagged wood everywhere. But it was what remained of the tree that commanded attention.

The top of the tree with a great percent of the branches had been blown off or burnt to cinders, but the trunk remained, having been ripped into equal parts. Unlike the leaves and branches, the trunk no longer burned and Steven was able to approach cautiously. From the house,he heard his dad shouting but it was only background noise.. The dying tree called to him.

As Steven neared, he could see the cream white center of the broken tree. It was beautiful and some parts looked as smooth as silk. But as he came closer still he saw that there was something out of place, something that must have been encased in the center of the trunk. As the rain continued to douse the fire and the heat level went down, Steven was able to step closer. Behind him, his ears registered the sound of the door to his home opening and closing but his full attention was on the tree.

The outside was burnt, but the wood inside, protected from the fire, gently twisted and Steven could see the golden grain clearly. At the center where the tree split down to the ground, was a doll. Not an action figure, not even a girl's doll, but a doll made of sticks and bits of cloth. A doll of wood and tiny leaves. The doll did not have eyes, but the minute empty sockets ordered Steven to act. Without a thought, he reached into the heart of the tree and plucked the doll from its encasement, stuffing it in his pocket.

"Steven," his dad hollered. "That damn thing could be dangerous. Get your butt over here!"

But the young teen could not take his eyes off the center of the tree. In the very center was the exact outline

The Doll

of the figure now in his pocket. It could be seen plain as day. But as Steven's father approached, his large feet squishing loudly on the lawn, the boy's eyes opened wide in disbelief as the wood liquefied and filled in the outline, solidifying again once it was gone. Steven rubbed his eyes. There was no sign that anything had been in the wood.

"Boy! What's the matter with...?" his dad began but his voice trailed off as walked up next to his son. "Good lord," he murmured. "That wood is...beautiful."

"I know," Steven breathed. "Look at it. And you know what else?" he said, turning to his dad.

"What?" his dad said, without taking his eyes off the tree.

No.

"Oh, um...look at how it's twisted. Isn't that cool?"

"That, Steven, is totally cool."

The street was beginning to come to life; neighbors came out of their homes to share in the excitement.

"Bill!" said Jeffery, a big fat guy, who lived across the street. "Say, Bill! You need me to call the fire department?"

Steven's father waved and replied. "Hey Jeffery! Naw, I think we're good. It missed the house, and it's out now."

Jeffery puffed as he plodded across the street. "Well Lordy, Lordy, Bill! That is a hell of a thing right there, isn't it? Damn lucky."

"Lucky is right Jeffery! Jesus, I could have lost the home."

Jeffery turned to the gathering crowd and bellowed in his bull-horn voice. "It's okay folks. No-one was hurt, and there was no damage 'cept to the tree." He turned back. "Well, Bill. I'm sorry about the beautiful tree but least you're safe. Now I gotta get some shut-eye. Got an early morning tomorrow."

"Sure, thanks Jeffery," Steven's father responded. "Thanks for coming over."

As the crowd started to disperse, Bill put a gentle hand on his son's should and turned him toward the house, where his mom, brother and sister stood. "Well, kiddo. Let's get inside. We can check this out more in the morning."

"Okay, dad," Bill said, running ahead. He flew past the rest of his family and into his room.

"It had to be my imagination," he murmured to himself as he slammed his door shut and sat at his desk. Slowly, carefully, he pulled the doll from his pocket. "It is a doll," he whispered.

It had not been his imagination. The doll was incredible in its detail. The tiny hands had fingers, and the arms seemed to ripple with veins. The face was blank except for the empty black eyes. Looking into them, Steven felt an oldness beyond anything he had ever encountered. It was a dark oldness, from the time when things began to grow. And it was full of hate. It was the doll that had ordered Steven not to tell his dad.

***

"And the tree just exploded!" Steven told the excited crowd at school the next day. "It was amazing. It broke right in half and was on fire, but the fire was put out pretty quick. There are a billion branches and leaves everywhere. My Dad said he is going to have to pay someone to come and take it away, but he is going to keep some of the wood from the center because it's so cool."

The Doll

"Aw, that ain't nuthin." Rich, a big kid, one or two grades ahead of Steven, scoffed. "We had a tree fall right on our house once. It was all flaming, and we had to call the fire department. I had to carry my sister out, or she would have died."

Liar.

"You're a liar," Steven said automatically, answering the voice of the doll in his pocket. He didn't know why but he had brought it with him to school. He had no intention of showing it to anyone. He just wanted it near.

"What did you say, you little fucker?"

Liar. Coward.

"I said you're a liar and you're a coward, too," Steven responded without conscious decision, his own eyes wide at his audacity.

The bigger boy began to grab for him, but Steven swatted his hand away.

The bell for the first class rang.

"This ain't over," Rick growled, pointing at Steven. "At lunch you are dead."

Steven knew that the large boy meant to make good on his word and began to sweat.

Calm.

***

Lunch came, and before he could even unwrap his sandwich, Steven was yanked off the bench by two meaty fists.

"Time to go to sleep you little fucker," Rich laughed. Three of his buddies stood behind him.

"Not here," one of them cautioned. "Back in the trees."

"Yeah," Rich agreed. "Not here. In the trees,we can

really work him over."

Rich and his friends began to yank and push Steven toward the trees that grew beyond the football field. Many a kid had received a good beating in those trees, and it looked like the same was in store for Steven. Behind, two or three gawkers followed.

Patience. Calm.

Once in the trees, they found a relative empty space out of view from the school. Rich pushed Steven to the ground.

"Now you're gonna pay, you little fucker," he roared as his friends laughed.

Steven stood and brushed himself off. He turned toward his opponent.

Begin.

"Let's get to it, then," Steven said calmly.

The larger boy looked at him in surprise but, even though he would have never picked a fight with someone his own size; Steven was much smaller, so he grabbed he younger boy's shirt with one hand and cocking back his other, he balled it into a fist...

Steven shot forward, and against his own will, kissed Rich on the cheek.

It only took a second and Steven had stepped back before either boy really knew what had happened. By the time the act had been realized, Rich was in full fury.

"You little queer!" he screamed, rubbing his cheek. "I am going to beat you so…"

Rich's words were cut off as he tried to take a step forward. He could not move. He looked down and found that vines had begun to grow at an amazing rate and wrap around his feet and calves. Worse yet, his shoes seemed to have exploded and his feet were busily growing shoots that were digging into the earth.

"What the...?" the boy cried, looking down and then he let out a horrible gurgle of intense pain as leaves began to grow out of his mouth and ears. He threw his head back looking upward and froze as bark and branches and leaves began to sprout from him everywhere.

The other kids, up to this time frozen in horror, began to scream and run.

No.

"Stop." Steven spoke. There was power in the word—a power of green fire and sunshine and growth that froze the children. One by one, Steven walked up to the kids and kissed their cheeks. By the time he had crossed back over the football field the clearing in the trees was no more.

It took a while to put it all together, but that night as his family lay sleeping in their beds, Steven knew. The lightning had released one of the ancient gods from the beginning of the world. It was the god of growing things, the god of green plants and sunlight, of rain and the seasons. And the god told Steven what every small child ever born knew instinctually.

Steven walked quietly out of the house, into the night and looked up at the stars. He walked over to where the tree had burned just the night before. Now there was just a stump, cut right level at the ground. Without a thought, he curled up on the stump, unfazed by the cold.

He knew that mankind was killing the world. The god reminded him of what he had forgotten with age. He knew there was no need to cut down forests. There was no need to cover the land with cement and glass and metal. He knew that there was no need to choke and poison the oceans with obscene liquids and waste. He knew that mankind had been given a chance; a chance to live correctly. But man had failed and had become an abomination. He knew that the world now hated mankind.

Steven fell into a quiet sleep on the stump.

***

Steven woke before the sun and found that a new tree had begun to grow out of the old, coming up between where he had curled and he saw that his own body heat had helped the delicate sapling grow. As he stood, he smiled at the beauty. He went into the house before anyone awoke.

At school that day, Steven, broke with his usual routine and methodically, class by class, kissed every student, teacher and administrator on their cheek. He had no hesitation or regret when he kissed his own sister on the cheek. He was simply doing what had to be done. By the time the school day was half over, no one remained inside and the building was being returned to the earth. By the time Steven had walked home, the school could not be made out at all.

"Hi honey!" his mom had greeted him happily. "Did you see the beautiful new tree growing in the front yard? It's a miracle. People from the paper have been here to photograph it... You're home early. Was it a half day today?"

"Yeah mom, school let out early. I love you," he said and kissed his mom on the cheek.

Marina Waiting

Vic Warren

Attendee: International Children's Book Festival
Bologna, Italy

New York 1953

Marina flicked the cigarette butt into the gutter. The current caught it and carried it down the block until it bobbed into the opening of the drain and disappeared. She lit another cigarette and looked at her watch. Eleven thirty. "Damn!" she said to herself. She bit her lip impatiently, and the tang of blood made her even angrier.

Late as always! She huddled tightly against the wall, trying to make the narrow awning keep at least a few drops of rain off her wool jacket, which was getting wetter by the minute.

A car drove slowly by, the slivers of rain gleaming in the path of its headlights. Its wheels sent out a spray of water that fell just short of her ruined high heels. Marina instinctively pulled her feet back against the wall and nearly fell, only staying upright by windmilling her arms and slamming one foot forward. The car's taillights faded as it drove on. Luckily, they hadn't seen her acting like a fool. She had dropped her cigarette which sizzled out on the wet sidewalk. Her stomach growled; she hadn't eaten anything since lunch. She looked at her watch again. One of Melchov Deli's skimpy pastrami sandwiches would seem like a feast right now.

Where in the hell are you, Joe? She pulled the pack of cigarettes from her purse. It was empty. *Shit!* She would have to kill him as soon as she could find him. The scum didn't deserve to live. She wadded up the empty pack and tossed it into the water, then stepped out into the rain and walked down the street, watching the wad of paper and foil as it sailed along with her.

Three blocks later, the lights from a late night diner shone out on the glistening pavement. Marina opened the door and stepped in, her shoes making puddles on the tile floor. The lights in the diner were blinding after so long on the dark street.

A couple sat at the fountain counter chatting and laughing quietly, and a lone man sat further down the counter. Marina sat down at a table for two by the window, and ordered a cup of coffee and a ham sandwich from the waiter. She got up and took off her wet coat, hung it over the chair at the other side of the table and brushed some of the water off its shoulders. Her blouse was damp, but the rain hadn't completely soaked through the coat. She went to the cigarette machine at the wall and bought a pack of Chesterfields, then walked over to the counter where the cook was making her sandwich.

"Do you have a pay phone?"

"Nah, but put a nickel on the counter and use the phone back there," he said, motioning to the back room shielded from the front by two swinging doors.

Marina found a nickel in her change purse and dropped it on the counter, where it clattered and spun to stillness. She pushed open the swinging doors and stepped into the dimness of the back room. The phone was on a table at the rear wall. She picked up the receiver, dialed EM-3486 and listened to it ring until she lost count of the number of rings.

The son-of-a-bitch is probably out, having a wild time with some floozy, she thought. She opened her purse, took out the little chrome-plated revolver and checked to make sure it was loaded, then picked up the phone again and dialed 0.

"Operator, would you connect me with the Yellow Cab Company?" She waited until the dispatcher came on the line, and then said, "I'm in a diner at the corner of Prince and Wooster. It's the only thing open. You can't miss it. Fifteen minutes? Perfect. Thank you."

She hung up the phone and returned to her table where her sandwich and coffee were waiting, picked up the mug and took a sip.

She took a bite of the sandwich. It was surprisingly good, made with plenty of ham and hot mustard, and she wolfed it down. By the time she finished the sandwich and coffee, and paid the man, the taxicab was just pulling up to the diner.

"Thanks," she said and put a dime on the counter for a tip.

"Thank you," he answered, putting the dime in his pocket. "I'm glad you've gotten yourself a cab. Nobody should be out there on the street on a night like this."

Marina ran out of the diner and crossed to the cab. It was raining even harder, and the drops pummeled her head and shoulders and bounced off the sidewalk and up her skirt. She pulled the door open and jumped into the back seat, slamming the door shut behind her.

"Ohh, will it ever stop?"

"Not tonight, Miss," answered the driver. "They're saying more of the same. Where to?"

"Do you know the Hickory House, on 52nd?"

"Sure, honey." He pulled away from the curb and turned left onto Bleecker, heading north.

Marina wiped the shoulders of her coat again and shook her hair to lose the worst of the water. She pulled out the Chesterfields, opened them and lit one, inhaling with a sigh. She glanced ahead but couldn't see any distance at all out the windshield. The wipers were in a losing battle with the rain, and she could tell that the driver was driving with extra caution, behaving nothing like a typical New York cabbie. She opened her purse and looked in her mirrored compact, then skillfully applied some lipstick. She closed the purse, then reopened it, pulled out the pistol and put it in her coat pocket.

The cab turned onto Broadway, then right on 52nd Street. Thanks to the rain, there was very little traffic, and they stopped in front of the Hickory House. Marina paid the driver and stepped out under the awning that reached all the way to the street from the club. What a relief, she thought. I'll stay dry all the way in.

The cop who walked this beat came towards her. He was dressed in a heavy black slicker and he held his nightstick, but wasn't twirling it with aplomb as he so often did.

"Well, sweep me off my feet," he chortled. "If it ain't me best girl, Marina."

"Hi, Billy. How have you been?" she asked.

"Y'know it's been a month o' Sundays," he said.

"Yes, I've been away for a while."

"Well, don't let me keep ya. Go on in, girl. I'd best be off into this fearsome night." And with that, he headed down the street, hunching his shoulders in under the pounding rain.

His name was really Officer Finnegan, but everyone called him Billy. He had been walking this beat for as long as Marina could remember. She had grown up just a few blocks from here, and when she was in school, Billy happily escorted the kids across the street, stopping the traffic with his nightstick like a flag. He was always interested in how you were doing, what you were studying in school. Over the years, he had been a real part of the neighborhood.

Marina turned back toward the door of the Hickory House just as it burst open. It was Joe, with a blonde in a full length mink coat on his arm, and they were enjoying themselves mightily.

Joe stopped dead in his tracks and stared at her. "Marina, you...."

Marina pulled out the gun and shot him three times. He crumpled to the ground, and the blonde screamed and backed away in terror as Marina looked around. She saw Billy running back toward her, and when he reached her, she handed him the gun.

"What on Earth, girl?"

"Just look at these shoes, Billy. They're ruined. And it's all that rat bastard's fault."

"I know you didn't shoot that man for a pair of shoes."

"No, of course not," she answered. "You've been around. You've seen how he treated me."

"Yes, Marina, I know that he's a low-slung dog. But just shooting him.... Well, come this way, then," and he led her to the club's door, stopping and bending down to check for any vital signs on Joe. They went inside, and with Billy's hand holding her arm, Marina began to slide in and out of consciousness. He put her in one of the vestibule's overstuffed chairs, and she slumped back into the comfort.

Billy asked Vince, the maitre d', for the use of a phone. He dialed the number and waited, then said,

"Sarge, it's me, Billy. I'm afraid I have some unfortunate news to report. Joe Vitello's been iced. Yeah. He's on the sidewalk outside the Hickory House. Better send Homicide, and an ambulance, before the body drives too many customers away. He ain't so pristine as he once was. Yeah, I got the shooter. No problem. And send a photog and the rest of the crew," he paused and looked at Marina.

"Yeah, I'll be a'waitin'. Mind you. Don't hurry too fast. We don't need no accidents in this muck. Hey, Sarge, tell Mikey he's a lucky devil. The body is under the awning, out of the rain." Billy smiled. "Sure, Sarge. I always try to do me best."

He hung up the phone and handed it back to the maitre d'. "Say, Vince, would ye be so kind as to get me a glass of water? And bring the young lady here something a little stronger. Make it a double, and put it on me tab."

"Marina, me dear," he said, shaking her gently. "Just you relax here a while. I'm going out to meet the squad car and the ambulance."

He took off his hat and ran his hand through the thinning white hair, then put it back on and swept out of the door in his oilcloth.

Vince handed Marina a double shot of whiskey, and she sat and stared at the brown liquid sliding between the ice cubes. She remembered earlier days when the sun shone and she was happy. How long ago was it? She took a large swallow of bourbon, and its burn woke her from her lethargy.

You stupid bitch, she said to herself, you've killed the schmuck, and now you're going to fry. She looked across the vestibule at the large, gold-framed mirror there. The woman in its reflection couldn't be her. She looked like a loser.

Sure, Joe was a loser, too, so why did I let him string me along? I could wash off my makeup and show the cops the mouse he had planted on me yesterday. I wonder if there's such a plea as long-term self-defense? They'd let me off if they could see all the bruises and the misery he's given me. How about the broken arm in April? Case dismissed, for sure.

She took another belt, started to cry, then slapped herself. Nothing but a goddamn victim! You deserve to swing, for stupidity, if nothing else.

The door opened, and a crowd of cops came in, Billy bringing up the rear. Two of them weren't in uniform, but Marina could smell Detective on their breath and see it in their eyes. The one in front, dressed all in brown and wearing a rain-dampened brown slouch hat, took one of the uniforms aside.

"Watch the door, Freeman. No one goes out or comes in, until we're done."

Vince came forward from his desk, "Is all this necessary, Lieutenant...?"

"Lieutenant Taylor. And yes, I'm afraid it is. You know there's been a bleepin' murder as well as I do." He stretched his hand, " And you are?"

"Vince Bonafides. I'm the maitre d' here at Hickory House."

"Well, Vince, I just want you to know that we won't be lingering. I promise you we'll be out of here just as soon as we can."

Billy drew up to the lieutenant, "See? What'd I tell you? Just look at the poor dear, crying from fear and distress."

The lieutenant sat down in the chair next to Marina, "There, there, little lady. From what I've heard you've had quite a shock."

"I, I…"

"You'd be cryin' too, Lieutenant, if your man had just tried to kill you," interrupted Billy.

Marina stared at Billy, and he motioned her to silence.

"It's Marina, isn't it?" asked the lieutenant.

"Yes." She looked for Billy, but he had faded into the background.

"Tell me, Marina, was Joe right or left-handed?"

"Left-handed. I used to kid him that was why he did everything wrong."

"And where did you get that gun?"

"Joe got it for me. He said it was for protection."

"And what did Joe say to you when you saw him outside the club?"

"He, he…"

"Ah, Lieutenant," said Billy, "I must apologize, but I can't let the sweet thing answer that. As far as I can tell, he said, 'Marina, you slut.' Forgive me, Marina, my dear."

"Is that right?" asked the lieutenant.

"I suppose so," answered Marina, looking down into her lap.

"Just ask Vince," urged Billy.

"Officer, I'm sure the lady is perfectly capable of speaking for herself," said the lieutenant. He turned back to Marina, continuing, "I'm told that he drew his gun, but the woman on his arm jerked away, giving you time to draw and fire."

"I don't know, I'm so tired," she cried.

"She had good reason to be afraid," said Billy. "Joe never did place much value on the lives of others."

The lieutenant put his hand on Marina's. "I don't want to upset you further, Miss, but I'm afraid we'll have to take you to the station."

Marina's heart fell. She pulled away and started sobbing again.

"No, no, it's only a formality. This is a clear-cut case of self-defense. We'll just need you to sign a few papers, and we'll bring you right back."

As they took Marina out to the squad car, its red rooftop light glowing, Billy waved after her. "Be brave, my dear," he called out.

The two cars pulled out into the rainy New York night, while the ambulance waited for the photographer to finish shooting.

Vince stepped up and put his hand on Billy's shoulder. "You sly old man. I saw you plant that gun on him."

"I didn't plant it, just moved it to its proper place, in his hand, not his pocket."

"Pretty risky stuff," Vince whispered. "What made you do it?"

"No daughter of mine is goin' to spend any time in the joint because of that slime."

"Daughter?! Does Marina know?"

"No. No one knows. And if you ever breathe a word of this to anyone, you'll be chum for the fishes in the East River."

Mr. Puselli's Rosebush

Jay Seate

Attendee: Starfest - Denver, Colorado

Mr. Puselli's Rosebush

In this age of Jesus sightings on a tree stump, the Virgin Mary in a piece of French toast, Elvis embedded in an orange peel, or the shape of the Elephant Man in an Idaho potato, I was aware of what one's imagination could concoct. But none of these oddities prepared me for Mr. Puselli's rosebush.

The gentleman arrived for his appointment at four o'clock on the dot. "Good afternoon, my two wild, beautiful flowers," he said jovially.

Not surprising monikers considering my name is Rose and my co-worker is named Iris. It was my week to draw blood from the bulging-eyed, corpulent Mr. Puselli. He suffered from an uncommon condition known as polycythemia, meaning too many red blood cells. The unfortunate fellow looked more frightful with each appointment, but year's ago when my prom date got drunk and spewed chunks on my high-heeled dance pumps, I'd learned to cope with unpleasant sights. I was a nurse after all.

Mr. Puselli's egg-yolk corneas were as unappealing as the rest of his face, swelled to the size of a beach ball. His extremities were bloated into spoiled, hairy sausages. He had an unusual explanation for his condition. He went on and on about alien close encounters. According to him, aliens entered his bedroom on a regular basis and put him through a series of tests culminating in injections which he felt certain were at the root of his circulatory distress. Iris and I dutifully nodded our heads and divested him of his extra cells. Unfortunately, we could do nothing about his overactive imagination.

We phlebotomized Mr. Puselli for months and, to the man's credit, he maintained a sense of humor, even though his thoughts continued to be fanciful and his words a might suggestive. During his last appointment, something brought out my antenna and suggested the visit didn't bode well for him or me. I wasn't afraid, just cautious. Iris and I often teased one another about whom Mr. Puselli had the biggest crush on, but our sarcasm and innocent barbs stopped abruptly when he missed an appointment.

As it turned out, Mr. Puselli had died from a clot in his brain the day after his last bloodletting. The rotund, little man had been particularly flirty and raucous that day in one final attempt to impress us with his randy wit. "I went to a shrink," he told us. "She claimed I had a split personality and charged me a hundred *samolies*. I gave her fifty and told her to get the rest from the other guy."

Iris chimed in. "I've got multiple personalities, so I'd only have to pay a few bucks, I guess."

Mr. Puselli appreciated our participation, but added cryptically. "It's the aliens that'll have the last laugh, I'm afraid."

The news of his death came just as Iris was lecturing me about the proper care of my flowering plants and my apparent lack of a green thumb. "You know what you need for your rosebush?" Iris had asked. "A few red blood cells. I poured the congealed stuff around my roots and everything perked right up."

We had no shortage of blood at the clinic, so at the end of the day, I pilfered a plastic bag from the freezer. "Come with me, Mr. Puselli. Part of you can still be

Mr. Puselli's Rosebush

useful," I wistfully said. "Your blood won't be missed, and you can help my garden grow, you poor man."

That very evening, I juiced my scrawny, blighted rosebush with Mr. Puselli's blood. I'd heard of people wrapping placentas around their bushes—the next best thing to having a dead body underneath my garden, but blood was gruesome enough. I took care to dig a trench around the bush's trunk and cover it with topsoil, hoping the neighborhood felines would not be attracted to the scent. The pint soaked in quickly.

As you've probably guessed, my rosebush turned from an ugly duckling to a healthy swan with shiny green leaves and velvety red buds. I actually gasped at each sight of them. They blossomed quicker than I thought possible into dark, crimson beauties. To be honest, they frightened me, and I hadn't been truly frightened since someone left a rubber finger sticking out of a sink drain in my middle-school's restroom. On that occasion, I screamed and peed my pants. I could only hope neither my mouth nor my bladder would betray me before *this* mystery was solved. Mr. Puselli's blood had certainly done the trick, but my rosebush revival had been too quick, too unnatural.

At one point, an interloper attempted to plunder the fresh soil. I heard a catfight, and upon investigation, found cat fur twisted around a thorn and droplets of blood leading from the bush to my cedar fence. "You're supposed to be poised and pretty, not a fighter," I told the rosebush. If not for a breeze murmuring gently amongst the floral inhabitants of my backyard, I would have sworn the plant sighed in response. *Don't encourage this bizarre rehabilitation*, I mused, and then felt foolish about my misgivings.

One evening, I stood at my kitchen window doing dishes as the setting sun cast its dying rays over the leaves and petals of my healthiest garden plant. The leaves had increased dramatically in size since I'd last taken notice. They didn't look like most rosebush leaves. They looked more like the spreading appendages of a maple tree. More like...hands with fingers. As I watched, two leaves trembled then closed in on themselves, opened and closed again as if beckoning to me, like the plant wanted to play patty-cake. I turned from the window stringing sudsy water across the counter and onto the floor. My breathing halted long enough for a train to pass. I had to remind myself to use my lungs.

This current situation wouldn't do. The corpulent rosebush was more than frightening. It was playing tricks with my psyche. The stories of Mr. Puselli's aliens reared their ugly heads. It didn't help that I was a sci-fi movie freak when I was a kid. Old memories die hard. All of his ramblings about aliens injecting experimental drugs into his veins gave me pause. Was there a connection to the way the bush was behaving? I'd believed the world my passionate Puselli lived in before he bought the farm was strictly for an old *Twilight Zone* episode. But now, my rosebush's blood-food was giving birth to a bizarro world more suited to *The Outer Limits* or *Tales from the Crypt*.

The flowers were so beautiful, much more so than its benefactor, rest his soul, yet so forbidding, so...sickeningly malevolent. Still, I couldn't bring myself to destroy this creation, but I *could* relocate it. I removed the plant from its sunny spot in my backyard to a dark, dank place on the north side of my home's foundation. Perhaps there, virtually without life-giving

Mr. Puselli's Rosebush

sunlight, it would wither and die. *Hasta la cucaracha*, baby. Its destiny was no longer in my hands but in Mother Nature's, I reasoned.

In its new location, Mr. Puselli's rosebush became a climber and leaned its thorny stalks topped by its perfect buds against the house. Stirred by the slightest breeze, the thorns scratched against the siding. *It's trying to get in*, I often thought. My most disturbing moments were when I took a bath. I somehow imagined my bathtub becoming the scene of a Hollywood horror cliché as an irrepressible plant stem found its way through the plumbing like a flower-tipped periscope in front of my painted seashell toenails. Perhaps the sight of me in the buff would scare it away rather than encourage a probe up my hoo-hoo. *Splish-splash.* At night, I tossed and turned in bed and pondered on how Mr. Puselli used to leer at me with those sad, bulbous features surrounding his bulging eyes. Perhaps my sleeplessness was more about his designs on Iris and myself than about aliens, but whatever the truth of the matter, this had to stop, beautiful roses or not.

Then the dreams came. Aliens had me. I lay naked on a slab. A woman with two heads and four breasts (Mr. Puselli always said he wanted to double his pleasure and double his fun, fondle two flowers instead of just one), was placing long-stemmed red roses into my…ahem, body cavities. In the background, I heard Mr. Puselli's familiar voice, extolling the virtues of his wild Irish Rose—that would be me. He pranced up next to the table on which I was splayed while being…decorated. He was also naked as a Jaybird. He was a human version of a cherubic Peter Griffin from the animated *Family Guy*, overly corpulent and covered with red veins pulsating with blood.

"Hello, my lovely flower," he said beaming. "A gardening you must go. My alien friends have planted the seeds. Now we can bloom together. Hardy-har-har." He was babbling like a dope head on a two-pipe high.

I fought at the stems, pulling them from my ears and mouth and ahem...other places, and awoke in a sweaty lather. Moving the bush hadn't been enough. More drastic measures were clearly necessary. I approached the rosebush with my trusty garden hoe and marveled again at the speed with which the stalks were climbing, topped by the furry flowers that were getting nearer and nearer my bedroom window. A large, gray tomcat as fascinated as I and apparently still drawn to the plant's scent, lay near the rosebush, flirting with danger. His tail whipped from side to side as if hypnotized by a hole full of mice.

"What's new, pussycat?" I offered.

The cat began to look dangerous.

"Get!" I hissed. Tom raised his hackles and lay his ears back, but refused to retreat. "Pssst," I added and raised the hoe. With a perfectly placed thrust, a swift jab at his furry *cajones* should curtail the romance between Mr. Tom and the rosebush. This proved unnecessary, however, for a thorny stem whipped against the cat's flank and brought forth a yowl of surprise. The cat looked at me with disgust then turned tail and ran.

Now, just the two of us, me and Mr. Puselli's rosebush, and the alien dreams given birth by my own plasma-pilfering actions. I came closer to the plush roses...too close not to see. "Walk away," my mind pleaded with my feet. "Walk away once and for all," but my body wouldn't obey. Curiosity of a cat, you might say. Even as my mind fought to reject the plant's latest behavior, my eyes saw.

At its base, the earth had softened and turned dark. Not from water. I hadn't watered since I'd carelessly replanted. The soil was too dark for water.

Blood!

The plant's root pulsated like a heartbeat. The topmost rose had fully blossomed. It was that flower which almost took away my rational world. Its blood-red petals lay open invitingly as I looked closer. *The Little Shop of Horrors* flashed across my mind. Audrey II had come from outer space, hadn't it? Within my little garden of horrors, Puselli's tale of infestation seemed more plausible than ever. My eyes blinked rapidly and grew hot. My saliva turned to sand. I was unable to speak. My hands were welded to the handle of my garden hoe. I couldn't look away from the bloom's revelation. Mr. Puselli's features rested within its folds. His gaping mouth lay between two rows of petals. Two raised, black spots on an otherwise unblemished petal were his bulging eyes.

I gawked, transfixed, and willed my body to respond. I knew I had to act quickly or forever be lost, pulled into Mr. Puselli's thorny caress. I raised the hoe and swung with all my strength. The blade caught the rose's stem, forcing it to the ground. The stem didn't break. A petal fell away…an ear. The plant's frenzied pulse raced through the stems to the other blossoms as they bent toward me. I placed my foot on Mr. Puselli's rose and raised my hoe again. A thorn somehow found my ankle and ripped the skin, but I was undaunted. Down came my blade a second time and severed the rose as I pitilessly ground the flower beneath my heel.

An internal scream exploded in my skull as the bush

sprang back to its upright position, spraying a thin line of crimson up my pant leg. The surviving uppermost rose seemed to unfold to its maximum circumference, replacing its fallen comrade. I stepped back, afraid to take my eyes from the plant as it replenished itself.

I thought of ways to destroy Mr. Puselli's rosebush but nothing short of pulling it from the earth by its roots would suffice. Perhaps, even then, the saturated ground would seed another unholy flora in its dark womb to pursue me.

Feets, don't fail me now. I ran from the scene and hustled back to the relative safety of my little cocoon. I closed my eyes afraid to see the images my mind was creating. I conceived of everything: dancing with a thorny rosebush that cracked jokes. Then I was floating in a vat of alien blood-stew along with poor Iris as our nipples turned into rose blossoms with Mr. Puselli's bulbous head and egg-yoke eyes floating between us in the steamy hot-tub from hell. Was it alien influence or Mr. Puselli's passion reincarnated? Whatever the case, I felt I had climbed aboard a rollercoaster ride leading to madness.

***

Yesterday, I did what I pray will let me sleep again. I gave a pint of blood at the clinic and brought it home. I dug a new hole along the foundation of my house. I buried the new plant and poured my blood around its roots, careful to keep it between Mr. Puselli and myself, while apologizing for my previous actions.

Will my new rosebush flourish and satisfy its companion? I can only hope the blood from one of Mr. Puselli's two "wild, beautiful flowers" might settle him down, but for now, I won't return to that side of the

Mr. Puselli's Rosebush

house and I've nailed plywood over my bedroom window.

And in case Mr. Puselli wasn't as far out there as Iris and I assumed, I've gotten new locks on all windows and doors in an attempt to protect against intruders looking for a new experiment. The worst thing is I think I smell dead cat outside, but so far, my mouth and my bladder are holding. Stay tuned.

Pesky Psychics

Lisa Ocacio

Attendee: Con on The Cob - Hudson, Ohio

Walter Simmons had been dead for ten years and had no interest at all in crossing over to the "other side." He was perfectly happy haunting the home he'd lived in most of his life. Only problem was, the house's current residents wanted him gone.

The house had changed hands three times since his death; no one seemed to want to live there very long. The new owners, Ted and Susan Weaver, had lived there about a month. Walter just didn't understand why they were making such a fuss. He didn't mind sharing his home and never did anything to frighten them. Well, almost never. They occasionally heard him walking around the attic, but who could be quiet all the time? And so what if he sometimes rearranged their furniture at night while they were asleep? It made the place look so much better, they should be thanking him. Instead, they were doing everything they could think of to get rid of him.

First, they brought in a priest to bless the house, but that type of thing only drove out evil spirits. Walter could admittedly be cranky at times, but never evil.

Next, they hired one of those new age people. She walked from room to room, chanting and burning incense, but only succeeded in setting off Ted's asthma.

Then began the parade of psychics; one by one they traipsed through the house, ranging in talent from those who couldn't "see" their way out of a paper bag to a few who could actually sense him. Walter found them to be the most annoying of all. They were all busybodies who should mind their own business and let a ghost haunt in peace. He did his best to ignore them and expressed his displeasure to the Weavers by hiding things like their eyeglasses or keys at every opportunity.

After a month passed without success, the Weavers seemed to abandon the idea of evicting him and the house became peaceful and quiet again.

Then one day, he wandered into the living room to find the Weavers having coffee with a young woman he didn't recognize. As he drew near, she suddenly looked right at him, smiled, and said, cheerfully, "Oh, hello, Mr. Simmons, I'm glad you could join us."

Walter froze, startled that she could see him.

"He's here with us now?" asked Susan, looking around wildly.

"Oh, yes," the young woman said. "He's standing right here, an elderly man, wearing glasses and a blue dress shirt with black trousers."

Walter groaned. Another blasted psychic and one with some real talent to boot. He thought they were all done with this foolishness.

The woman stood and faced him. "My name is Megan O'Reilly. The Weavers are disturbed by your presence here and have hired me to help you move on. I can show you how to reach the other side."

"I'm not interested in going anywhere. This is my house. If they're not happy here let them 'move on'," he said, grumpily.

"Now, Mr. Simmons, that kind of attitude isn't going to help us resolve anything."

"You can hear him, too?" Ted asked, incredulously.

"Ask him what he did with my car keys."

"Hush, Ted!" Susan snapped. "Don't interrupt Megan while she's working."

"Oh, it's all right. We're just getting to know each other. Isn't that right, Mr. Simmons?"

"How do you know my name?"

"I did my research," she told him. "There's only been one reported death in this house, a man named Walter Simmons, who lived here for fifty-three years before passing away from a heart attack. I can only assume that's you. Am I correct?"

"Yes," he admitted, grudgingly.

"Great! Can I call you Walter?"

"No."

"How about Walt?"

"No!"

"Wally?"

"DEFINITELY NOT!"

Megan signed. "Fine, Mr. Simmons it is then. May I ask why you don't want to want to go to the other side? You'll find peace there."

"It'll be peaceful here once you leave," he replied, irritably.

"I'm only trying to help you."

"I don't need your help. Go away!" That said, Walter disappeared to the attic where he could be alone.

The next day, he went to a local movie theater that was showing a classic western marathon. The man taking tickets shivered as Walter passed right through him. One of the perks of being dead was that he never had to pay for anything.

He was halfway through the first movie when a familiar voice whispered, "Hi, Mr. Simmons. I love these old movies, don't you?"

He turned to see Megan seated next to him, calmly munching popcorn. Walter groaned in annoyance.

"How did you find me?" he asked.

"I'm psychic, remember? It was easy."

"Shouldn't you be in school? How old are you anyway? Fifteen?'

"I'm twenty-five, Mr. Simmons, and I have a degree in parapsychology."

"Para-what?"

"Parapsychology, it's the study of unexplained phenomena." When he still looked confused, she added, "like ghosts."

"Oh."

He noticed their fellow movie patrons were glaring and trying to shush her.

"Doesn't it bother you that everyone around us thinks you're a crazy person, who's talking to herself?"

She shrugged. "I'm used to it. If I stopped to explain myself to every person who thought I was crazy I'd never get anything done. But enough about me, I'd like to know why you're still here."

"Are you planning on talking through the entire movie?"

"If you have unfinished business, I can help you resolve it."

"There's nothing to resolve, I just don't want to go."

"Why not?"

"It's none of your business!" he replied, testily, and left her sitting by herself.

On the third day, he found Megan sitting alone at the kitchen table, drinking coffee.

"Good morning, Mr. Simmons," she said, cheerfully.

'How are you today?"

Still annoyed with her for ruining his movie marathon, he barely grumbled a reply. He was disappointed to find her there now. The Weavers were at work and he was hoping to have the house to himself for a while.

"Isn't it a beautiful day?" she continued, undaunted by his grumpiness. "But you know what's even more beautiful? The other side. You'd see that if you just gave it a try."

"You just don't know when to quit, do you?"

"I only want to help you."

"Like I told you before, I don't need any help," he said. "Go bother some other ghost."

"What about friends and family who have died? Don't you want to see them again?"

"There's no one I care to see on the other side."

"Really? Are you sure? What about your Mom and Dad?"

Walter snorted. "My mother left when I was four and my father was a mean drunk, so no."

"Oh," she said, "I'm sorry to hear that. You must have had a very difficult childhood."

He shrugged self-consciously. "Yeah, well, I got over it."

"I see," she said. "Hmm, my research said you were never married, but there must have been some special lady in your life that you'd like to see again."

"There's only one woman I've ever really loved. Her name is Evelyn Rainfield and she's still very much alive."

"How do you know?"

"Now that I'm dead I think I'd feel it if she died, too.

There was always a strong connection between us. See, we were high school sweethearts and very much in love, but her parents didn't approve of me. I was from the wrong side of the tracks and they forbade her from seeing me. We continued our relationship in secret for a while, but then one day her family moved away and I never saw her again." He didn't know why he was telling her all this. He hadn't liked talking about it even when he was alive.

"We kept in touch through letters, and though I dreamed of marrying her one day, in reality I knew I didn't have much to offer her. I was barely making a living back then and she deserved so much better. So, as much as it pained me, I started to encourage her to move on and find someone else. She didn't want to give up on me, but I really felt it was for her own good. I wanted her to have a happy life, even if it were without me, so I eventually broke off all contact with her. I never forgot her though, and I still think about her almost every day."

Megan sniffed and wiped her eyes with a tissue. "That is so sad."

"Yeah, well, it was a long time ago and what's done is done."

She brightened suddenly. "Hey, maybe you should go find her."

"What do you mean?"

"I mean you could be with her again. There's nothing holding you back now. Since you're still stubbornly refusing to cross over to the other side, you might as well find some peace here by being with the woman you love."

"What good would that do when she wouldn't be able to see or hear me? Besides, it's been so long; I'm sure

Evelyn's forgotten all about me."

"You never forget your first love, Mr. Simmons." Megan told him. "You certainly haven't forgotten her and so what if she can't see or hear you? You'll still be with her and I'll bet she'll sense your presence. Plus, you'll be out of the Weavers' hair. It's a win-win!"

Walter had been giving her suggestion serious consideration until she mentioned the Weavers. "Oh, I get it. This is a trick," he said, angrily. "All you care about is getting me out of the house, so you can get paid and build your precious reputation."

"That's not true!" Megan protested.

He ignored her. "Well, your plan's not going to work! This is my house, and if the Weavers don't like living here with me then they can dang well move somewhere else! Now that's what *I'd* call a 'win-win'." And with that said he vanished in a huff, leaving her stammering in the kitchen.

The next day, he expected to find Megan waiting for him again and had planned on giving her the cold shoulder, but, to his surprise, she was nowhere to be seen. Nor was she there the following day or the day after that. When a week passed with no sign of her, he figured she'd finally given up. *Good riddance,* he thought, but after two weeks had gone by he actually started to miss her a little. It had been nice to have someone to talk to for a while, even if she had been an annoying pest.

Then one day, out of the blue, she was back.

"Hi, Mr. Simmons, did you miss me?"

"No," he lied. "I was just starting to enjoy the peace and quiet again. What are you doing back here anyway? I thought you quit."

"I never give up that easily, I just needed some time to do some research," Megan said, cheerfully. "How'd you like to take a little road trip?"

"Road trip? To where?"

"It's a surprise."

"No, this is another one of your tricks to get rid of me. I'm not going anywhere."

"It's not a trick, Mr. Simmons, I swear," she said, exasperated. "I've never done anything to try to trick you. In fact, I'll make a deal with you. You come with me now, no questions asked, and afterwards, if you still don't want to cross over, I'll never bother you again."

"You promise?"

"I promise," she said. "I'll even try to talk the Weavers into leaving you alone, too."

He could never pass up an offer like that. "Alright," he said.

It took a lot of concentration for Walter to remain solid enough to ride in Megan's car, but he eventually managed it. He was very curious about where they were going, but he'd agreed not to ask questions, so he merely stared out the window and enjoyed the passing scenery.

They drove through the country to a small private hospital. There, Megan led him to a room where an elderly woman lay on the bed. Megan approached her and gently touched her arm.

"Mrs. Foster?" she said, quietly. "It's Megan O'Reilly, remember me? I'm back and I brought him with me this time."

The woman turned her head toward them and opened eyes that were the clear blue color of a bright summer sky. Time seemed to freeze in that moment as he looked into the face of his beloved Evelyn. Even after the passage of so many years he would know her anywhere. She was still so beautiful.

"It took me a while to find her," Megan said. "She's here under her married name."

Evelyn was looking at him. "Walter? Walter, is that you?"

"She can see me?" he asked Megan in surprise.

"Yes, and hear you, too," she told him. "I'm afraid she's dying, Mr. Simmons, and the closer someone is to death, the easier it is to see spirits. I'm sorry to have to tell you this, but I don't think she has too much time left."

Walter stepped toward the bed. "Yes, Evelyn, it's me."

"I heard you died."

"I am dead," he said, then added quickly, "but don't be scared, I'm not going to hurt you." The last thing he wanted to do was frighten her.

To his relief, she smiled, weakly and said, "I know that." Then she frowned. "But you did hurt me once, Walter. You broke my heart. Why did you end our relationship? We could have been so happy together."

"At the time, I thought I was doing the right thing. I had so little to offer you, I thought you'd be better off without me."

"I never cared about how much money you made. We would have gotten by. I just wanted to be with you."

"I'm so sorry, Evelyn," he said. "I realized later what a huge mistake I'd made, but by that time it was too late. You'd already married someone else."

She nodded. "I waited a long time for you to change your mind, Walter, but I couldn't wait forever. I was lonely, and Howard was a good man. We were married for over ten years, but eventually it all fell apart and we ended up getting a divorce. I tried really hard to make it work, but he just wasn't you."

"It's so good to see you again, Evelyn. I've missed you so much. Not a day has gone by when I didn't think of you."

"I've missed you, too." Evelyn smiled, and then she closed her eyes and sighed. Walter and Megan jumped as the alarm on the heart monitor suddenly went off.

A nurse rushed in, checked on her patient, and then called for assistance over the intercom. As she began CPR, she told Megan, "I'm sorry, Ma'am, but you'll have to leave the room."

Megan left as a group of nurses and doctors came rushing into the room. Walter stepped back but didn't leave. He watched anxiously from the foot of the bed as they worked on resuscitating Evelyn. Then suddenly she was standing beside him.

Confused, she looked from him to her body on the bed and asked, "What's going on?"

"I think you just died," he said, gently.

"Really?"

"Well, I don't think its official until they stop working on you. You might still have a chance to go back."

"Oh," she said, thoughtful. Then she looked earnestly up into his eyes and asked. "What if I don't want to go back?"

"It may not be entirely up to you," he told her, casting a meaningful look upward.

"Oh," she said again, glancing up as well. Then she took his hand, and they stood together, waiting and watching as the hospital staff worked to revive her. Ten minutes passed, then fifteen. They tried valiantly, but after twenty minutes they finally admitted defeat. Evelyn was declared dead and covered with a sheet. Sadly, they gathered their equipment and filed out of the room. Walter could hear them talking to Megan in the hallway.

Evelyn was staring at the bed. "This is very strange." Then she turned to him and asked, "What happens now?"

"Wait for it," he told her.

"Wait for what?" Then she gasped in surprise as the white light appeared. "Is that what I think it is?"

"Yep."

"It's so beautiful."

"Yes, it is," he agreed.

Megan came back into the room. "The light is here for you, Mrs. Foster, but you can both go into it."

"Both?" Evelyn asked, looking confused. "Walter, when you died didn't the light appear for you?"

"Yes."

"Then why didn't you go into it?"

He shrugged. "I guess I just felt like there wasn't much for me on the other side. Everything I ever really cared about was here," he said, and then added quietly, "including you."

"This is your chance to be together again, Mr. Simmons," Megan told him, "and this time it will be forever."

Evelyn turned to him and took his hands in hers. "I want to go into the light, Walter, and I want you to come with me."

He looked into her eyes. "Are you sure? We could always stay here together."

"I'm sure. We've lived our lives and now its time to move on."

Walter took a step toward the light, then turned and looked back.

"Its okay, Mr. Simmons," Megan said. "I'll make sure the Weavers take good care of your house."

He nodded. "Goodbye, Megan. You've been a real pest, but you brought Evelyn back to me and for that I'll always be grateful."

"Yes, thank you so much," added Evelyn.

"You're very welcome," Megan replied, smiling.

Hand in hand, they stepped toward the light, but just before they disappeared into it, Walter turned and said, "Oh, and tell Ted his car keys are in the fish tank."

Consequences

J. M. Vogel

Attendee: Marcon - Columbus, Ohio

"You're late!" Levana's eyes blazed, as Al jetted through the door, sweat pouring from his brow.

He threw himself into the chaise lounge and readied himself for work. He felt silly calling it that, but that's really what it was. Levana fed off him and then paid him for his time. Work. Sometimes the fact that work felt almost like a sex act made him feel like a mimbo or gigolo, but only sometimes. He only had to remember unemployment and living with his parents to set him straight. She was his employer and he her employee. And right now, his employer was angry and hidden somewhere in the dark recesses of her very plush office.

"I'm very sorry Levana. I..." He paused unsure of how to proceed. Could his lunch with Allie be considered a breach of contract and therefore punishable by death? He'd been a little foggy when he'd signed that part of the agreement with his own blood, having just experienced a feeding session with Levana. From what he remembered, he was not allowed to enter into a relationship with anyone unless he wanted to die. But where was that line? The cute girl with the red hair and pixie features who'd nearly mowed him down in the middle of the road wasn't his lover -- yet. She'd just taken him to lunch as an apology. Sure, they'd had a great time and, yeah, he'd fought the overwhelming urge to kiss her good-bye, but that wasn't anything that warranted his death. If only he'd ended it there.

Enthralled by her gorgeous green eyes and unable to refuse, he'd accepted an invitation for drinks on Friday. The fact that he even considered what it would be like to see Allie naked definitely pointed to the fact that the line he shouldn't cross was quickly approaching.

"Yes? You were saying?" Levana prompted, her voice sharp. The rustle of Levana's long, flowing gown across the plush carpet signaled her approach long before he could see her. Now a few months into their arrangement, he'd never seen her in anything but curve-hugging, velvety dresses. As she exited the shadows and glided into the dim light,he was once again struck by her beauty. She was truly a sight to behold – even angry.

"I was almost killed."

Levana raised an eyebrow. "Really?" she asked, oddly intrigued. She placed her soft, delicate hands on his head and tousled his wavy brown hair. His pulse began to race as he anticipated what came next. She was slowly draining his very soul from his body, and generally he just could not bring himself to care. Today, however, something was different. Doubt began to nag at the corners of his mind. Perhaps he hadn't given this arrangement enough thought.

"Oh, yeah, I can feel that," she purred as the tiny tentacles on her fingers suctioned to his scalp. His heart began to beat in double time and his breaths came faster and shallower. Pleasure the likes of which he'd never experienced before Levana overtook him as he settled into a worry-free haze. She began to sigh as the feeding intensified. "Fear...intense fear," she said gripping his skull. "Oh, what is this?" she asked.

Al froze. From the tone of her voice,he could tell she was sensing something she hadn't expected. Emotions, to

Levana, were seasoning for her meal. Apparently she'd found a new one. But what could it be? Could she somehow sense he'd been with Allie this afternoon? "What is it?" he managed to croak out.

"Anger. Doubt. Confusion. Remorse." She nearly squealed with delight. Apparently his internal conflict was appetizing. The feeding suddenly reached an intensity it never had before, and Al lost all semblance of reason. He rode the wave of ecstasy until Levana removed her fingers from his scalp. He lay in the chair exhausted yet satiated without a thought in his head.

"Wow you were simply...delectable today," she sighed as she slumped back in her chair. Al, still fuzzy, could really only see her face. The rest of the dim room was a blur. "Oh...apparently I indulged a little too much," she said, rising over him. "Are you alright?"

Al opened his mouth to speak, but words wouldn't form. He was transfixed by her orchid stare. Normally the fact he couldn't speak would concern him, but he was so dazed he couldn't bring himself to care.

She nudged him toward the edge the chair, slid in beside him and placed two fingers to his neck. "Well, your pulse is still racing, but it is steady. You should be alright in a few minutes. I apologize. I usually don't lose myself that way. You just tasted so good."

It took about a half of an hour for Al to recover most of his faculties. After some mental gymnastics, he was able to pull himself up to a seated position.

"Finally," Levana sighed. Al looked around the room, but couldn't see her. She emerged from the shadows holding a small glass of amber liquid. "Here, drink this."

Al sniffed the glass. Brandy. He shook his head and

gestured for her to stop. "No thank you," he managed choke. He'd had a rough night with brandy right after his ex-wife moved out and had no desire to ever touch the stuff again.

Levana insisted. "It will help. You and I, Albert, need to have a chat."

Al's heart began to race again. "About what?" What if she'd sensed the attraction he'd felt for Allie? Or the murderous thoughts he'd had when he realized he could only have Allie if Levana was dead?

"About our arrangement."

His muscles wound themselves tighter than a drum. His eyes scanned the room but nothing dangerous or deadly was in sight. Then again, if she were going to kill him, she'd only need to place her hands on his head and feed off him until nothing remained. He shivered at the thought. He had no idea how to injure a being like Levana let alone kill her. He pressed the snifter to his lips and drained the glass. The brandy burned like acid all the way down, but slowly his muscles unwound. "What about our arrangement?"

Levana perched herself next to him on the chaise. "We've been at this for a few months now and I think it is important to set expectations."

Al nodded. "Shoot."

"The first few months, as I explained in the beginning, are a honeymoon period. A compatibility test if you will. Luckily, you passed with flying colors so I don't have to kill you. But, as I mentioned in the ad, this has the potential to be dangerous work. Today's feeding let me know that we are ready, compatibility wise, to go to the next step."

Al gulped. "Next step?" In his ignorant bliss, he'd

become complacent. All of the warm fuzzies he'd been getting from the feedings had made him forget the ad altogether, let alone the caveat about danger. He'd convinced himself this was it.

"Today I went overboard because it is the first time in months I'd had a taste of something new. I just couldn't help myself and, as such, I nearly rendered you brain dead."

Al tried to remember the feeding and the aftermath, but everything was murky. He had no idea he'd come so close to losing it all.

"The way to avoid this is to give me variety. If I am trying something new frequently, I am less likely to indulge in such depth."

Al raised an eyebrow. "And how do I do that?"

Levana's purple eyes glittered. "I am going to start sending you on assignments. Uncomfortable assignments. And when you return, I will feed."

While her words seemed innocuous enough, the message behind them made him wary. "Like what?"

One corner of Levana's mouth tugged up into a half smile. "We'll start easy. I'd like you to go to a bar and seduce someone. Tomorrow."

Al's ears perked up. He was already going to a bar tomorrow to meet someone. It seemed too easy. "You want me to start dating someone?"

Levana rolled her eyes. "No. You know that's not allowed. I want a one night stand or as close to a one night stand as you can muster."

Al's mouth dropped open. She was giving him permission to go out with Allie. He must have misunderstood. Could it really be that easy? "I don't get it."

Levana stood and paced slowly around the room, as if orating a speech. "There are a lot of emotions that go into meeting and seducing someone new. I will need you at the normal times for breakfast and lunch, but I don't want to see you until the deed is done. Once your encounter is complete, I want you to come here, regardless of the time. I'll be waiting."

After a few more instructions, Al left Levana, his mind heavy. He trudged to his car and started it up with none of the joy or excitement that usually accompanied driving. His first purchase upon accepting Levana's employment was to buy a new car. Normally, he'd fire up his brand new BMW convertible, crank the stereo and hit the gas. He loved driving that car, happily shifting through the twists and turns on his way to and from work. Today, however, his brain was too taxed. He didn't even turn on the radio for fear that adding even one more thought to his mind would cause his head to explode. He rode in silence all the way home.

What a weird freaking day. When Al left for work this morning, all was right with the world. Everything was in order and made sense. Within the span of a few hours, his world had been turned on its ear. His mind was a jumble with thoughts of Allie and Levana; and his new job description. Only one thought continually floated to the top of the mire – *why did I take this job with Levana?* He fell asleep on his couch pondering that very question.

***

"This isn't a good idea. We probably shouldn't see each other anymore," Al said, watching himself in the rearview mirror. "That's not it," he sighed. His fists pounded the steering wheel in frustration. He'd been practicing what to say the entire way to the bar and for the last fifteen minutes while parked outside in the parking lot, alone. He didn't understand why he was having such a hard time rejecting a girl that he'd known for all of a few hours.

To say that Al had thought a lot about this situation over the last twenty four hours was an understatement. He'd obsessed over it. But after weighing the pros and cons over and over again, only one solution made sense – he simply couldn't start anything with Allie. He'd given up that option when he'd signed on with Levana and, regardless of how he felt about that decision now, there was no going back. Plus, he didn't want to die. The sane and rational way to achieve that end was to march into the bar and let Allie off the hook. Given the kind of life he was living, he was actually doing her a favor. Then, after she left, he could do as Levana instructed and pick up some floozy for a one night stand. Al sucked in a breath, hit the steering wheel one more time for good measure and headed for the door.

***

What did I do? Al asked himself. He looked across the bed at the beautiful redhead asleep beside him. He'd gone to the bar that night with the best of intentions. *How did it go so wrong?* He knew the answer to that question before he could even finish the thought – he'd fallen for Allie. As soon as he saw her perched on that barstool with her cute little grin he was hooked. And apparently, she felt the same way. It didn't take long for the two of them to find themselves in the parking lot and all over each other.

"What are you thinking about?" Allie yawned. She reached out stroked his bare chest.

"Just how unexpected this all is."

The corner of her mouth pulled up into a grin. "I know what you mean," she agreed.

"I mean, I thought I was done with women. I never in a million years even dreamed I'd find anyone I'd want to be with ever again." *If I had, I'd never have signed up with Levana* he added mentally. If he even suspected he'd find someone like Allie he'd never have signed his life away. What a mess he'd made of everything. And now he'd brought Allie into the mix. Even through his divorce and unemployment he'd never loathed himself as much as he did this instant. He had to find a way to fix this, and if that mean that Levana had to die, so be it.

As if she could read his thoughts, his cell phone vibrated on the night stand. "I'll be right back," he said as he grabbed the phone and headed to the bathroom.

Once he was safely behind the bathroom door and out of Allie's sight, he read the message from Levana:

RETURN TO ME IMMEDIATELY, REGARDLESS OF WHETHER YOUR TASK IS COMPLETE.

He leaned over the sink and, for the first time in months, caught a glimpse of himself in the mirror. He didn't even recognize the man who stood before him. After only a few months, he was visibly older. Faint lines were forming under his eyes. It wasn't significant yet, but his face looked as if it were starting to sink in ever so slightly and the hair above his temples showed just the beginning of gray. But these slight physical differences weren't what alarmed him. What scared him beyond belief was that he didn't recognize the man behind those features. In fact his eyes didn't even look like his own anymore. They look cold and dead. He splashed his face with water and thought of what lie he'd have to tell Allie so that he could leave. He hated it, but it was the only option now. When he'd formulated the best lie he could, he left the bathroom and headed out to Levana's.

***

"Were you successful?" Levana asked as he entered. She was sitting by the lounge chair ready for her feeding. Apparently she was hungry. For the first time ever, she wasn't wearing her trademark style of dress. She wore jeans and a t-shirt, her black hair tied up into a ponytail. It looked good on her. But even with the common clothes, she wouldn't pass for the girl-next-door. She was still somehow exotic.

He nodded in answer to her question. When he considered his "success" he suddenly felt ill. He thought of Allie's face as he told her there was an emergency at work...at two in the morning. He saw the doubt and betrayal in her eyes as he pled his case. He wasn't lying after all, or at least that was how he consoled himself the entire way to Levana's. But Allie wasn't dumb. She knew there was more to the story than he was saying. He didn't think he could face her ever again.

Levana was short on patience. "Sit down, sit down," she directed hastily. "Let's get started, please."

Al slumped into the chair and closed his eyes. The excitement and anticipation he normally felt before she fed was completely gone. Levana put her hands on his head and gasped. "Wow. So much emotion!"

The feeding seemed to take forever. Levana took her time as she relished his misery. When she finished she stood up laughed. "You really are a sap, aren't you?"

"Excuse me?"

She giggled and headed to the bar for a drink. The lights in the office were higher than usual and he could see her clearly as she poured herself a glass of wine.

"You hook up with some bimbo and have very satisfying intercourse if I am reading your emotions correctly, and then fall in love with her in the span of a couple hours?"

"No I didn't," Al bristled. She was right and he knew it, but he didn't like how she spoke of Allie. She wasn't a bimbo or a floozy. She was trusting and good and kind and he slept with her, knowing all the while that he couldn't have a relationship. He'd essentially taken advantage of her. The fact that Levana was feeding off of that interaction made it so much more wrong. He hated her.

"Well, from the look on your face I can tell the love you're feeling isn't for me. Goodness gracious Albert, do you ever feel anything but angst? I should have realized that on that first day when I sensed just how desperate you were that you were someone who was prone to baggage. I should have put you out of your misery right then and there."

Anger boiled just beneath the surface. "You need to stop," he growled.

She was visibly taken aback by his sudden anger, but not intimidated. She threw her head back as she laughed at him. "And you're going to make me stop how?" she mocked.

That was all it took. Al charged her. He'd never hit a woman before but Levana wasn't a women. She was a beast. An abomination. Unnatural. He lunged at her, his fists ready. He'd never felt so much raw anger before. He pulled back, ready to smash her condescending face, but his arm stopped in mid-swing and he flopped to the ground, helpless. Levana had managed to get a hand on his arm before his fist impacted her face. The tentacles latched on and he was completely vulnerable. She'd apparently been holding back during their feeding session because in the span of a second, he was incapacitated on the floor and unable feel anything. Blinding rage to numbness in one second flat.

"This won't happen again, Albert...Unless I choose for it to happen of course. There is something appetizing about this level of rage. You're lucky I'd already eaten before you pulled this stunt. You might not have made it."

Al lay shivering on the floor. "I want out, Levana. I don't want this anymore."

Levana crouched down beside him and stroked his face with the back of her hand. "Oh, Al. You know that isn't how it works. You're mine. For life."

"Then kill me. Now. Put me out of my misery."

Levana rolled her eyes and stood. "So dramatic. What amazes me is that the thought of losing your 'soul' as you call it gave you no pause whatsoever. But a pretty girl bats her eyes at you and suddenly this arrangement is intolerable. You humans and your priorities."

"Please, Levana. I can't do this anymore. Please, kill me." He never meant anything more in his entire life. He couldn't go on this way.

Levana placed her hands on her hips. "Well this is wholly unattractive. Get yourself together, get up and get out of my sight. I will not kill you until I am ready to. At this point, I've put entirely too much work into this arrangement, and I will not start the process over because of a case of puppy love."

Al pulled himself to standing and trudged toward the door.

"Oh, Al, I almost forgot. Your assignment for tomorrow."

Al turned to face her, defeat and self-loathing evident in his face and posture.

"I want you to mug someone."

"What?"

"I want you to approach a stranger and take something from them by force if necessary. I don't care what you take, but take something."

"I...uh...no...well..." he was so discombobulated by the request that he couldn't form a coherent sentence to voice his opposition.

"Spit it out," she sighed.

"I can't do that. I could be arrested."

"Well then be smart about it. You've given me quite enough to chew on today, so I don't need to see you until tomorrow night after you've completed the task."

"No. I won't do it." He stood tall and confident, very aware of the line he was drawing in the sand. Either she'd let him out of this task, or she'd kill him. One way or the other, he'd have won some small part of himself back.

"Aren't you cute," she chided.

"No. I'm serious. I will not rob someone. It's wrong." He crossed his arms over his chest.

"Oh, now you're concerned with right and wrong. What a convenient set of morals you have. I'll tell you what, Albert. You do have an option. You can do as I tell you or you cannot. But I promise you this, if you do not follow my instructions I will kill you...but only after I've killed this girl you are so smitten with. And, I'll make you watch. And don't think she's safe in her anonymity. I have my ways of finding out. I always find out."

Instead of getting a little back, he was risking more every minute. Without a word, he turned his back on

Levana and left. With every day that passed, Levana's death was more and more of a necessity. He spent the rest of the night on the computer trying to figure out how one goes about killing a succubus.

***

"Give me your wallet," Al growled as he stuck a squirt gun in the back of a twenty-something male. He was in a dark alley on the fringe of the local college campus. So far this evening, he'd *not* robbed a high school girl, an elderly man, a pregnant lady or a man with his young son who'd chosen to walk through this very dark and desolate passage between two busy streets. Figuring that the college-aged kid would be the least traumatized by his attack, he covered his face with his hood and lunged at him just after he'd passed. The young man willingly gave up his wallet and ran away. Al took off around the corner and tried to disappear into the crowd on the street. It wasn't long before he realized his was being followed. He prayed that it wasn't by the police.

Once he was free of the crowd, he disappeared around the corner and leaned against the building, lying in wait to see the face of his pursuer. Seconds after he popped around the corner an all too familiar face turned on him and proceeded to punch him square in the stomach.

He grabbed her wrists before she could sucker punch him yet again. "Allie! What are you doing here? It isn't safe!"

Tears were streaming down Allie's face as her eyes met his. "I know. I saw that poor boy you just mugged."

Al fought the urge to puke. He'd never wanted her to see that. He didn't want anyone to see that. "Allie, it's something to do with…work. I really can't explain."

Allie screamed in frustration. "You mean like that work emergency that called you out of bed at 2am?"

"Yes! Just like that. Allie, it is really complicated."

Her lips tightened and she gulped back a sob. "I'll bet it is complicated. Your wife probably thinks so too."

Al's mouth fell open. "Allie, no. That isn't how it is. I'm not married."

Her eyes fell on the ground as she spoke as if she were ashamed. "I followed you that night. I don't know why I did it. We'd only just met and I know I was dumb sleeping with you on the first date and everything, but I felt something. Something I've never felt before. And you looked so upset when you left that I was worried, so I followed you."

Al cringed. "What did you see?"

"I followed you to West Maple and saw you duck in a building. I waited outside, in an alcove. You were in there for what felt like forever. When you came out, you walked right past where I was standing. You were muttering about her. You smelled like her. You were so angry, I just put two and two together. You just don't get that angry about someone you aren't involved with."

Al put his hands on her shoulders and felt her shudder beneath them. "Please believe me. I am not romantically involved with her. She really is my boss. And we were fighting because she is trying to make me do things I really don't want to do. Like rob that kid tonight."

Allie stepped back, away from his grasp. "Then quit."

Al slid down the wall and placed his head in his hands. "It's not that simple."

Allie threw her hands in the air, exasperated.

"No, really. Levana is..." he paused, struggling to explain. "This is going to sound dumb, but she isn't human. I ended up taking the job a few months back after I'd basically given up on anything good ever happening again." He knew this all sounded so ridiculous, but he just didn't care. It felt good to get it all off of his chest. "She's turning me into a monster and I hate it. She is literally sucking the soul right out of me."

Allie looked doubtful. "What is she?"

Al shrugged. "A succubus? Maybe?"

She rolled her eyes at him. "Ok, let's pretend I believe you. What does she have on you? Why can't you leave?"

Al looked up into her green eyes and hesitated. "She's holding something over me."

She shrugged. "Like?"

Al warred with himself. Tell her or don't tell her? In the end, he was laying his cards out on the table, so he might as well go all in. "You. She said she'd kill you if I didn't comply...and then she'd kill me."

Her eyes bulged with surprise. She was silent for a long while as she considered the situation. Al stood and leaned against the wall while she processed. After a few quiet minutes,Allie stopped pacing and met his gaze. "Well then, I guess we're just going to have to find a way to kill ourselves a succubus."

Al had never been more attracted to anyone in his whole life.

***

"Where have you been?" Levana growled, impatiently. "Surely it didn't take you this long to find someone to burgle."

"Well, believe it or not, I'm not a career criminal. So

yeah, it took some time." What he of course couldn't tell her was that he'd spent the last hour and a half with Allie, plotting and planning. They hadn't come up with an answer yet, but just knowing they were working towards his freedom gave him hope.

Levana scowled. "You are getting dangerously close to needing disciplined, Albert. Now, have a seat so that we can get started."

Al wasn't sure what Levana would sense from this feeding and he really didn't care. He was riding a high from his conversation with Allie and from the freedom he felt with everything being out in the open. He sat down in the chair and closed his eyes. This could be one of the last feedings he'd ever have to endure. He cleared his mind and waited for her to place her hands on his head.

"You're much more docile than last night, Albert. Hopefully that means you've accepted these new duties." She placed her hands on his head and instantly, Al felt relief wash over him. He hated it, but he couldn't hold on to the anger. "I just want you to know that this is all part of the adjustment period. This conflict happens with each feeder to some lesser or greater extent. You'll come around."

He really hoped that wasn't the case. He wanted out as soon as possible.

"Albert, are you still in love with that girl?" she asked as he felt the feeding intensify.

"No," he said through gritted teeth. Levana was doing something different; she was exerting a kind of pressure as if she was trying to push the emotion from his body.

"Here, let me take care of that for you," she said as

she turned up the feeding yet another notch. "I can make you feel better."

"No, please," Al begged before his thoughts began to jumble. Suddenly out of the corner of his eye he saw Allie, her eyes wide. She looked shocked and appalled and scared all at the same time. He wanted to yell for her to get out of there, but he couldn't. His whole body was gyrating and he felt as if he could pass out at any moment.

As she watched Al convulsing uncontrollably, her face contorted into a mask of anger. Levana's attention was diverted by her intense feeding—she didn't notice Allie creeping up behind her. Allie grabbed a bottle of alcohol from the bar and doused the back of Levana with its contents. Levana's head whipped around, but before she could even mutter a word, Allie ignited the rear of Levana's dress with butane lighter.

"NOOO!" Levana screamed repeatedly as she fell to the ground attempting to smother the flames. As she rolled on the ground, Allie grabbed more bottles and one by one emptied them each onto the writhing Levana. With each bottle, the flames grew higher until the shrieks and screams stopped and the fire engulfed Levana's whole form. Allie let it burn a little longer than she should have, but she wanted to be sure that Levana was no more. Al watched as she calmly and methodically put the fire out with the extinguisher from the wall. Only after each and every flame died did she stop moving.

"Wow," Al said as he tried to will himself to get up. Levana had taken a lot from him, but not so much that he couldn't move this time. He stood and walked toward Allie who stood frozen staring at the pile of ashes. "That was impressive. How did you know what to do?"

She simply stared at the pile of ash, her eyes the size of dinner saucers.

Al put his arms around her and she collapsed, unable to support her own weight. He pulled her tightly to his chest and let her sob. After a few moments she pulled away, wiping the tears from her eyes. "I'm sorry. It was all just so intense. I've never done anything like that before."

"But you were awesome. Thank you, Allie. Thank you for setting me free." He moved toward her, but she stepped back from him."

"Allie, what's wrong? We can be together now."

Tears streamed down her cheeks as she mechanically shook her head back and forth. "No. We can't."

"Why not? Levana's dead. Please Allie. I know it's only been a short time, but I think I'm in love…"

Allie interrupted him before he could finish the thought. "Stop. Don't say it. I've seen too much. I can't un-see what I walked in on just now. You were enjoying it, Al. You were enjoying her touching you. And even worse, I killed her and not just because she was evil. I killed her out of jealousy and anger. You talked about how she was turning you into a monster, but you turned me into a monster and I just don't know how to deal with that."

"What are you saying, Allie? You don't want me?" Al asked, his heart in his throat.

"I'm saying I need space. I don't know if I'll ever get past what happened here tonight. But every time I look at you I'll see her and I don't want that."

"Come on, Allie. Please," he begged. He deserved to be alone and he knew it. But while it was true they'd only just met, somehow, he just couldn't imagine his life without her.

"Good-bye, Al. And good luck." she said as she walked out the door.

Al plopped down in the chair and looked around the office. Levana was a pile of ashes and no longer in control, but she was also no longer his meal ticket either. Without a paycheck, he could say goodbye to his house and car. Allie was gone, so he was completely alone. How eerily familiar this all felt. The only thing missing was plans to live with his parents.

Just then his phone rang. He looked at the caller ID and sighed.   "Hello, Mom."

"How are you Albey?"

"I just lost my job."

"Oh honey, I'm so sorry. Do you need a place to stay?"

Perfect.

Screams in the Night

J. P. Behrens

Attendee: Camp NECon - Bristol, Rhode Island

Strange symbols glowed with a red-orange aura pulsing around Father Loren. Twisted figures writhed in the darkness, smoky, golden explosions tearing into them. Terrible screams from adults and children assaulted Loren's senses. He clutched a small child to his chest, protecting it from the horrors slithering in the emptiness. Loren called out, telling the victims to be strong, that he would find them. He *would* help them. A wet, gurgling laugh was the only reply. Loren prayed, his black rosary moving quickly through old, gnarled fingers, but God didn't answer. Not that he expected Him to.

Blood curdling screams woke Loren from his already disturbed dreams. He exhaled a soft, awkward chuckle for being so disturbed by nothing more than fantasies induced by a troubled subconscious. It was only after Father Loren realized the screams continued into wakefulness that dread colored his drowsy perception. While wiping the sleep from his eyes, Loren fumbled for his glasses on the nearby nightstand. Outside his door, he heard the frantic commotion of heavy footsteps up and down the hallway. As Father Loren reached for his robe in order to investigate, a loud knock shook his small boarding room's door.

"Father! Please, quickly."

The voice belonged to the young man who had helped carry his bags only a few hours ago. Loren couldn't recall the boy's name; only that he was determined to leave Arkham behind and had a kind soul. Now he hammered away, panicked, at Loren's door. After a disorganized attempt to clothe himself, Loren opened the door to see a sweaty, stricken face.

"What is going on?"

"The woman next door is having a fit. We need your help with her."

"I'm a priest, son, not a doctor."

Another scream tore through the paper-thin walls of the dilapidated boarding house. Loren thought the place a deathtrap, but it was inexpensive and he only intended to stay the one night.

"I know, Father, but we need you. Please, come and see."

A tired sigh escaped Loren's lips as he exited the room. The boy tugged Loren's arm as the two moved down the aged, nicotine-stained hallway toward the source of the wailing. Loren lost all control of his legs on entering the room. Each wanted to collapse and run at the same time. His mind skirted the edges of madness. The horrific scene before him was more than an epileptic fit. It was insanity made manifest.

The screaming came from an elderly woman, the maid by her uniform, curled up in the corner and tearing at her face. All around her, chunks of flesh stuck to the floor. The maid kept fighting whatever terrifying hallucinations assaulted her, alternating between flailing at the air and clawing the grisly remnants of her face. The old woman's eye sockets were bloody holes, mangled by crazed desperation. Though blinded, the visions must have remained, for the self-mutilation continued. Blubbering in the corner was a large man mumbling incoherent nonsense. Loren recognized him as the owner of the establishment. There was a fetid puddle of urine and filth forming beneath him. The owner's eyes fixed on the young girl standing in the center of the room. Before Father Loren could speak, the girl flickered across the room towards the deranged innkeeper, sidling up beside him. She whispered briefly in his ear. The screams that exploded from the innkeeper drove Father Loren from the room. Behind him, Loren could hear a deep, malevolent chuckle.

Father Loren involuntarily passed his hands in the sign of the Cross, praying silently for God to protect him. The young man pursued Loren into the hallway. Still reeling from the short visit in the room, Loren stumbled backward into one of the walls. Loren collapsed onto the floor, oblivious to his surroundings. The only thing he could see was that room and the girl.

"Are you ok, Father?"

"I... I don't know..."

"Can you help?"

"I've heard stories about things like this... Just stories."

"Father, please."

Loren looked up into the young boy's face. It was pale with desperation.

"What's your name again, son?"

"Wally, Father."

"Wally, please call your local priest. I'll possibly be needing his help."

Wally shuddered, his fingers twitched as he spoke. "You mean the Catholic priest?"

"Of course, son."

Wally dove down the hallway. Loren thought Wally's last question a peculiar one, but shrugged it off as a momentary lapse. Picking himself up off the floor, Loren made his way back to his room. When he shut the door, the screams from the room were muffled. If only he could believe it was just another guest watching a horror movie too loudly. The bed looked inviting, but duty called him elsewhere. A mirthless laugh escaped his lips. Training for this sort of thing was limited and rarely taken seriously by those not specializing in it. He knew the words, the actions, the theories, but the idea of performing an exorcism on a possessed child was too much like a movie for him to believe. He had been a priest for most of his years and never had he heard of one real incident. But, those two people driven mad, that girl's supernatural movement, and the evil laugh that pursued him from the room were more than he could ignore or deny. Something unwholesome was occurring in the small boarding house. Loren feared he might be the only hope they had, unless the resident priest could be persuaded to take care of the problem.

Rifling through his bags, Loren found an old copy of the *Rituale Romanum*. Slipping the tome from amidst the other worn religious texts, he rushed across the room. He snatched up the small note pad and pen provided by the boarding house. On the writing table stood a stack of newly procured arcane texts, which a professor from Miskatonic University left to the Church. The letter that had come with them warned that none of the texts should be used without extensive study. The books discussed, in great detail, a number of strange, possibly evil, rituals. Pulling his gaze away, Loren began leafing through the *Rituale Romanum*. He quickly found the section dealing with exorcisms. He jotted down the required items as neatly as his shaking hands would allow. When Wally came back, Loren handed him the list, emphasizing the need for expedience. Wally nodded, scanned the list, and nodded once again to himself as he dashed off to gather the supplies.

Father Loren looked around his room in the strained silence. During his preparations, the screams faded away. Loren looked at his wall, willing himself to see through all the plaster and wood. Instead, the small plastic crucifix hanging over his bed stared back. Loren could remember the peaceful years as head of his church, giving stirring homilies, providing a soup kitchen, and even started starting a popular youth Bible study. After the shooting in the Church day-care, however, he just couldn't look into the eyes of all the mothers and fathers who asked why. Why would God allow some crazed gunman to take their babies? Unable to provide answers, he rededicated himself to research. Loren felt a man shouldn't proclaim the greatness of God while harboring an irreconcilable anger.

The sad look in Jesus' eyes made him think of everything he had lost. That little girl in the other room may not be able to find salvation in the Lord, but he would not abandon her to the whims of dark forces. He straightened his creaking back, washed his face in the small bathroom basin, and finally donned the cassock, the crisp, white collar, and the silken stole. He hesitated when his eyes fell on the rosary, a gift from a little old lady, Grace, who was his first parishioner. Loren had used it when performing her granddaughter's confirmation, then again for her wayward son's baptism after that stint in rehab, and finally for her Last Rites. There were other rosaries given to him by bishops and other grateful families, but this one was special. It was one of the two items he couldn't bare to throw away during his crisis of faith. It was more than a symbol of his faith in God. It was a symbol of his faith in people. Loren wrapped the rosary tight around his right hand, clenching it over and over, hoping it would give him the strength to get through the night.

Loren exited his room. Wally shuffled up the steps carrying a small, cardboard box filled with the exorcism supplies. Loren watched a small, greasy-haired man lurch into view behind Wally. He was dressed as a Catholic priest, but his vestments were graying and worn. The dingy stole hung limply over his shoulders, frayed at the edges, and wrinkled from prolonged storage. The resident priest lazily looked up and down the hallway, found Loren, and unhurriedly walked toward the senior clergyman.

Loren's first impression of the man was not flattering. The young priest's eyes were sunken. His jaundiced skin stretched over abnormally shaped bones. A thin-lipped smile revealed brown stained teeth too thin and long to belong to a normal human being. Loren took the priest's hand in greeting. He nearly recoiled at the slick, clammy grip that enveloped his hand. Those long, slender fingers seemed to go on forever. If Loren didn't know better, he would have sworn the priest's hand was actually a mythical demon growing out of his arm like some miniature Hydra of Greek legend. Fighting the urge to run into his bathroom and scrape away the memory itching over his hand, Loren motioned for the man to follow.

"Hello, Father Loren, is it? I am Father Marsh."

"I understand the oddity of all this, but we definitely have something unnatural on our hands. I was hoping that you might know the parties involved and maybe even take control of the situation. I am not accustomed to this sort of thing."

"What sort of thing would that be, Father?" Even his voice was sickeningly slick. "An exorcism."

Marsh chuckled. "I know we here in the New England area have a strange and somewhat colorful reputation, but I doubt this is anything more than some poor woman's psychotic episode."

Instead of arguing, Loren thought it better just to show him. Once at the door, Loren paused. Silence met the duo. A sense of foreboding seeped from the room. Loren willed his hand to turn the knob. The door cracked to let the light spill into the hallway.

The room was deathly calm. The innkeeper and maid were no longer there. There was no evidence that anything unnatural had happened. Father Loren inched into the room. The girl slept in her bed, content and peaceful, nothing amiss. Loren immediately rushed to the corner the owner had crouched in. No puddle or stain remained. It was as if nothing happened. While Loren ransacked the room for a sign of the maid or owner, Marsh slipped into the room. His expression resembled the bored patience one reserved for a child who saw monsters under his bed.

Offering a kind, soft laugh, Marsh consoled the priest. "The boy must have heard the girl having a nightmare. You woke abruptly, saw your own nightmare, and over-reacted. I'm sure it was just your research getting to you."

Nodding, numb from uncertainty, Loren allowed Marsh to guide him back to his room. Trembling, Wally watched from the darkened staircase. Loren wished to comfort the boy. He wanted to ask how Marsh knew about the research or even the nightmare, but confusion fogged his mind. The adrenaline from recent events vanished, leaving Loren drowsy and easily maneuvered. Loren barely heard Wally's pleading whimpers as Marsh ushered him through his door.

"Get some rest, Father. I'll keep an eye on the girl for the night while I look into where her family might be. You just forget about this whole mess and sleep."

Loren accepted the suggestion, rested his head on the pillow, and lost consciousness as Marsh exited the room. Before sleep took him, Loren kissed the rosary still wrapped around his hand and mumbled a short prayer for Wally's soul. If asked later, Loren would not be able to say why he felt the need to do so, but would be glad the words were spoken.

Frightful dreams assailed Loren's sleep. The girl's face hovered innocently before him. Blood-covered tentacles writhed beneath her. Strange appendages with small gapping mouths lined with teeth snapped at the air. All the while, still worse mutations crept below, distorted under liquid darkness. A long, slender tentacle wrapped itself around Father Marsh. The two merged, obscuring where one began and the other ended. The girl's face loomed closer, whispering dark words. Marsh smiled with mock patience, amused contempt obvious in his assurances that everything would be okay. As the girl opened her mouth, Loren could see Wally, trapped within the endless pit of her gullet. His pain-twisted scream resonated until it filled Loren's entire being. Before the scream could reach its mind-shattering climax, the girl snapped her jagged teeth shut, smiling in the oblivion.

Loren fell from his bed with a panicked shriek.

His heart pounded beneath his breast. Grabbing a loose end of the bed cover, he mopped his forehead, amazed by the amount of sweat pouring from him. He slowed his racing heart by counting the rosary beads still entwined around his hand. Creaking joints bitterly reminded Loren of his growing frailty. Loren's throat was hoarse from screaming. He stumbled across the room. The water pitcher on the desk was empty. He located the phone and lifted the receiver. It automatically began ringing the front desk. The trilling continued without answer for far too long. Wally should have picked up the line. Loren felt very cold as he recalled the dream and Wally's tortured scream.

The cobwebs of sleep slowly dissolved as he crossed the small room. Cracking the door to the hallway, Loren peered out. Nothing moved in the corridor. The lights seemed weaker than earlier. Some flickered, determined to fight back the invading darkness. Loren stepped out into the empty space and looked down the stairs.

"Wally?" he whispered into the darkened lobby.

No answer.

Loren squinted into the shadows but discerned no movement. The deafening silence drummed on his mind. Something was off. While crossing in front of the girl's room, he caught a glimpse of something caught in the wooden frame. The flickering lights glinted off the object, making it hard to identify. Loren pried the object from the wood and began to fiddle with it. It was sticky on one side, leaving behind a residue. Horrified, Loren realized what was in his hand. He swatted at the torn bit of fingernail, trying to free himself of the vile remnant. Retreating back to his room, Loren covered his mouth to stifle the scream rising from his soul.

A quick prayer spilled from Loren as he turned on the small lamp at his desk. His vision was plagued by black and white dots flashing across his eyes. Loren calmed himself, heartbeat by heartbeat, once again using the beads of the rosary as touchstones, but as normalcy tried to piece back together the framework of reality, a small prick stabbed at his arm. He looked over his sleeve to discover the bloody fingernail. Panic flooded back in, allowing a hysterical shriek to escape. Loren, however, recovered from the abyss of madness to pick the disgusting, ungular barb from his clothes. A dry swallow punctuated the light tick as the nail fell from his fingers onto the enameled desk. Staring at the dark red smears coating his fingers, Loren remembered the vivid dream, Wally's scream still echoing in his mind.

Unable to hold it back any longer, Loren keeled over and wretched into the small dustbin beside the desk. The warm, acidic taste coated his mouth until he spit out the last bit of vomitus. Falling back, weak from the effort, his attention fell on two books, the *Rituale Romanum* and a curious notebook that had been obtained with the various rare texts left to the Church. Having little time before leaving Miskatonic to study the notebook, he recalled mention of a spell that would summon powerful, ethereal beings.

A dry heave exploded from Loren. Panting for breath, Loren pulled himself up off the floor. Right in front of him was his bag of religious texts. The words *Holy Bible* stared at him. The book was small and humble, a gift from a much-respected teacher. After the violence of the world invaded his life, corrupting his faith, it was the one touchstone that reminded him why

Screams in the Night

he followed the calling into the priesthood. Loren needed that memory now. He pulled the book out, set it down with the other two and made a decision. Trembling at the thought of confronting what was going on in the boarding house, Loren unearthed an old strength thought lost to the past, embraced the books to his chest, and marched out into the hallway.

The once dim hallway was now swallowed by darkness. Lights still flickered but provided only feeble illumination. With each flash, small details twisted from familiar to distorted. Paint melted away, then rippled and undulated. Hands stretched from beneath the wallpaper, tentacles lashed out, the ground quaked one instant only to sink and squish under foot the next. The hallway took on a gory, organic appearance. Father Loren concentrated on breathing, ignoring the suffocating metallic odor oozing from the throbbing walls. Before long, he reached the door leading to the possessed girl and the almost certainly deceased Father Marsh. Loren reached out. The doorknob disappeared, transformed into a small orifice which flexed outward, devouring the screaming Loren.

Reality snapped back into place. Disoriented, Father Loren nearly toppled over. Attempting to brace himself, he found the solid support of the bathroom door handle. It twisted under his weight, throwing him forward once again. Loren stumbled further into the room before finding solid footing. The stains from the owner and the maid were once again visible. Fresher remnants of macabre acts marked the room. Father Marsh kneeled beside the bed, whispering strange words reverently while the child examined Loren. She smiled at him, brilliant white teeth flashing in the light, reminding him of the disturbing dreams that began this cursed night.

"Demon, I shall cast you out. May the Lord protect me—"

The girl cackled at the priest. "Demon? Oh, my dear, old man, I am so much more than that. Your God has no providence over me. In this battle, priest, you are very alone."

"If you are not a demon, what?"

"You saw in your dream. Am I not glorious?"

"How—?"

"Is not important. Soon this world will become ours once again. The Old Gods will rise. The Elder Ones will once again roam this planet. The vermin that infest this realm will be swallowed by our arrival. Reality will once again bend to our will, and this time, nothing will end our influence over this existence."

Loren struggled against insanity. His hands tightened on the rosary. The beads bit into his flesh. They reminded him what was real and who he was fighting for.

The supplies for the ritual had disappeared with Wally, but Loren needed to keep going. Once the book was opened to the exorcism spell, he began. The Latin rolled off his practiced tongue. The little girl only giggled at his desperate attempt. By now, Father Marsh had finished his prostrations. He stood by the bed, a twisted grin distorting his features.

"You are a priest, Marsh. Help me stop this madness," begged Loren.

"I told you this wasn't an exorcism, you old fool. Stop it? We have been awaiting this for centuries. Many have come close, but none has succeeded until now. Just imagine, an Old One hidden within a human vessel. In the past, there were complications, mutations if you will. But this time, we will finally bring an end to this diseased world. The Elder Gods will cleanse our world of the weak, and we shall be elevated to gods for our loyalty." As each word tumbled out, fanatical zeal burned brighter in Marsh's eyes.

Loren glimpsed alien, writhing movement under the sheets. "Mutations?"

The girl patted the twisting appendages. "Yes, well, I can't be in this disgusting form when my brethren arrive."

As if on cue, a high-pitched wail pierced Loren's mind. Blood-soaked visions of a Cyclopean world inhabited by lumbering monstrosities invaded his thoughts. Pain, pleasure, hate, love, lust, greed, and vengeance all mixed together into an amoral morass of philosophical identity. Whatever these beasts were, they were coming. Loren remembered the notebook. Though the letter strictly prohibited him from using any of the spells without thorough research, there was no choice.

He crouched down in the corner, repeating prayers taught to Sunday school children, flipping through the notebook looking for anything that might prove useful. The other two creatures across the room no longer concerned themselves with Loren, assuming he was driven mad by the visions of the world's destruction. Loren was frenzied, yet a small corner of his mind still soldiered on, fighting to find some way out. A piece of yellowed parchment slipped out of the book to the floor. Loren snatched it up, reading the scribble.

Could it be true? Should it be done? Audacious, dangerous, pompous, but to actually meet Him?

Loren flattened the book to insure he did not lose his place, chipping large chunks from the delicate edges. The Latin script was faded but still legible. Loren choked, shaken, as he read the words that invoked, no demanded, the presence of God. Still staring at the blasphemous spell, Loren heard the hungry, gnashing howl echo closer. There was no time.

Loath to do so, Loren swiped his fingers through one of the many blood trails still soaking the carpet and found a clean area to create the arcane symbol needed to focus the spell. Reading the words, at first low and soft, his voice grew in strength with each recitation.

"What is he doing?" Loren heard the girl hiss. He couldn't worry about them any longer. He needed to finish. "Stop him, fool! He will kill us all."

Marsh dove across the room, his claw-like hands stretched out and ready to squeeze the life from Loren's frail body. Loren, without stopping the spell, screamed the final words as he snatched a pen from the nearby desk and drove it into Marsh's scrawny throat. Though Marsh's hands found their target, blood poured from the wound, weakening him enough that Loren was able to fight free.

Silence overcame the room. Not even Marsh's dead body made a noise as it flopped to the floor. Loren looked around, dreading that the walls of reality were crushed, that beasts beyond description were now gathered around him, drooling, sniffing, relishing the first kill they would have after an eternity of exile.

Instead, he found a being of light standing before him. The girl hissed and thrashed at the newcomer. It merely stood there, analyzing the room. Its robes were made entirely of starlight, blazing brighter and hotter than any fire made by man, yet cool in the glow bathing Loren. Tears rolled down Loren's face, joyous rapture crushing both heart and soul. God had come in answer to his summons. Surely, his hubris would be forgiven in light of the dire circumstances. The sight was more fulfilling than any modern day miracle of faith or science. Loren, for the first time in his life, knew what it was to be completely at peace.

The feeling was short-lived.

The God-being turned to look at Loren. It was a sight that would haunt him for the rest of his natural life. All of his joy was replaced with revulsion. There was nothing human about the creature that looked down on Loren. Its eyes were swirling black pits, sucking in all the light that emanated from the robes. It had no mouth, only two black, hungry eyes. Its skin slithered unnaturally over its form, constantly slipping and twisting. Only those soulless chasms remained fixed.

It turned back to the girl. As Loren's summoned creature lifted its hand, two large talons were exposed. Something more moved within the confines of the long robe, but all Loren could see were the claws.

"You should not have come back, Old One."

Without replying, the human shell exploded. A mass of tentacles and teeth lashed out, attacking, whipping at the being Loren had summoned. Before anything could reach the faceless creature of light, a swirling void opened up behind the slime covered mass and pulled the bloodthirsty monster out of Loren's world.

"Thank you—"

Loren's voice cut off as the creature turned its emotionless gaze on him.

"Do not speak to me, worm. I should rend your very soul from this plane of existence for summoning me here."

Loren blinked in confusion. No words came from his

gaping mouth.

"The Old Ones are nothing to me. This world is nothing, merely one floating rock amidst an ocean of galactic splendor. This realm is but one among an infinity of others. How did a primitive like you call me here?"

Loren felt his throat loosen. "I didn't mean to call you. The spell said it would call God, the Creator of All. I am His priest. I am sorry if I offended you."

"I have no need of priests. How did you call me here?"

Loren lifted the small piece of paper from the floor. Before he could offer it to the being as apology, it burst into flame, same as the symbol smeared into the carpet.

"Do not disturb me again."

Loren thought it best to remain silent and picked himself up off the floor. Only something had struck him odd. "I'm sorry, but you said you have no need of priests. What did you mean? I am a priest of the Roman Catholic Church. I am a servant of God and his son, Jesus Christ."

A long silence forced Loren to search deep into the endless pits.

It answered, "I have no need of priests or servants, especially the residual afterbirth of a failed experiment."

Loren collapsed to the floor. As the being dimmed, receding to nothing, Loren gaped, desperate to process what the creature meant, to find a way around what that thing had just revealed.

From a life begun in the abject service to God, to surviving the devastating attack that claimed the lives of many children and his faith, to the adulation of being so close to his perceived creator, Loren's world came crashing down with just six, simple words. *I have no need of priests*. All meaning in life and creation was turned to ash with a simple explanation of the human condition.

Loren reached up slowly, hooked the now filthy collar around his neck, and pulled it away. It fell to the floor with no more than a whisper, settling beside his old, worn Bible. Both symbols of his shattered faith remained on the blood soaked carpet as Loren limped out of the room. He went back to his room and found a candle he had kept as a gift from a Bishop who helped him during his crisis of faith, guiding him to a life of research— beginning the path that led to this night of dark enlightenment. Loren found a box of matches in the desk and lit the candle. He watched the flame flicker, considering everything he had just learned, then set the candle on the ground next to one of the flimsy curtains. As the flame caught the dingy lace, Loren emptied all his priestly garments into the growing blaze. He considered taking some of the books he acquired at the Miskatonic University with him instead of consigning them to the flame. They represented what could be the only truth left in the universe, but he turned away without regret. His heart could not handle any more truth than what had been pressed upon him so recently.

The flames blazed into the night, casting a blood red haze over the path leading Loren into darkness. As he walked away from the cursed boarding home, Loren unconsciously mumbled a litany of simple prayers to himself as the beads of his rosary fed through restless fingers. It was still hours until sunrise, and when it came, the old man would barely notice or care. Only the sounds of prayers learned by rote and the clicking of beads filled the air. One for each sin committed in the shadows of the moonless night.

Author Bios

"Preacher Con" - Lyndsey Davis

L. R. Davis writes fiction and non-fiction from children's fantasies to apologetics, and spends too much time on the computer, so enjoys walking to compensate. A retired Navy chaplain, she pioneered in the women-at-sea program. Her Honors B.A. in English and M.Div. in Theology, strengthened writing for newspapers, magazines and Seasons of the Church. http://www.lyndseyrosedavis.weebly.com and blog at http://www.lyndseydavis.blogspot.com .

"Shelter" - Leo Norman

Leo Norman lives in Southampton, England with his wife, Emma, and son, Elijah. He loves stories of the supernatural and monsters because of what they reveal about our real lives. He has previously been published in Sanitarium Magazine.

"Whitechapel" – Monica Cook

Monica Cook is an American-born freelance writer based in Adelaide, Australia. She is a history devotee and incorporates historical events and settings into her fiction. In between writing short stories and working on her first fantasy novel, Monica is studying a Master of Writing degree. Monica belongs to several online groups dedicated to the Harry Potter and Dr Who fandoms.

"Skin and Bones" - Kyle Yadlosky

Voodoo, sideshows, and a good ghost story—if it's outside of the everyday, Kyle Yadlosky revels in it. He lives in between corn fields in Pennsylvania and has been published in Smashed Cat Magazine, 69 Flavors of Paranoia, Gone Lawn, and Mad Scientist Journal. For more of his stories, you can check out kyleyadlosky.tumblr.com.

"Red Cove" - Michael Mohr

Michael Mohr is literary agent Elizabeth Kracht's assistant (Kimberley Cameron & Associates). In addition to writing a regular blog (Michaelmohrwriter.com) about the industry, Michael is a published author. Find his work in Flash: The International Short Short Story Magazine; The MacGuffin; the San Francisco Writers Conference Newsletter, and as a guest blogger in Writer's Digest. He lives in Oakland, California.

"Origins 1995" - Kathleen Molyneaux

Kathleen Molyneaux is a recovering academic living in Cleveland Heights, Ohio. She has a Ph.D. in Cell Biology. Her work experience includes the care and feeding of yeast, HeLa cells, frogs, mice, whooping cranes, cats, and humans. She is currently working as an Ultrasound Technician. She writes science fiction and mysteries in her spare time.

"The Doll" - Patrick Van Slyke

Patrick Van Slyke grew up in the shadows of the Big Horn Mountains in the small town of Sheridan Wyoming. An avid reader, as a child he was drawn to fantasy and science fiction. He attended the University of Wyoming and it was here that his love of Horror began. Patrick now lives in California with his daughter and fiancé.

"Marina Waiting" - Vic Warren

Growing up in Seattle, Vic Warren attended San Francisco Academy of Art before working as an advertising executive in the travel industry. He is best known for creating the Alaska Airlines Eskimo logo. He produced more than 100 children's books and has written three suspense novels, Stairway of the Gods, Saffron and Hong Kong Blues. He lives in Kailua-Kona, Hawaii with his wife, Laurel.

"Mr. Puselli's Rosebush" - Jay Seate

Jay Seate writes everything from humor to the erotic to the macabre, and is especially keen on transcending genre pigeonholing. Over two hundred stories appear in magazines, anthologies and webzines. Homepage: www.troyseateauthor.webs.com.

"Pesky Psychics" - Lisa Ocacio

Lisa Ocacio is a retired nanny. She enjoys writing short stories about ghosts and is currently working on her first novel, which is full of magic and superheroes. "Pesky Psychics" is her first published work. She lives in Brunswick, Ohio with her husband, father, and cat, Zatanna.

"Consequences" – J.M. Vogel

J. M. Vogel lives in a suburb of Columbus, OH. She is setting out to show the world that a degree in English does not predestine you to life in the unemployment line. Keep up with J. M. Vogel by following her blog at http://jmvogel.blogspot.com.

"Screams in the Night" - J.P. Behrens

A storyteller most of his life, JP Behrens has weaved an intricate web of bold faced lies, some of them in the form of stories. Life is a learning experience, and he's tried to learn from both wondrous successes and miserable failures. Though JP has managed to fib less often, he still tells the occasional exaggerated tale here and there.

Coverart: "The Doll" – Luke Spooner

Luke Spooner a.k.a. 'Carrion House' currently lives and works in the South of England. Despite regular forays into children's books and fairy tales his true love lies in anything macabre, melancholy or dark in nature. He believes the job of putting someone else's words into visual form is a massive responsibility, as well as being something he truly treasures.